QUINX

by Lawrence Durrell

QUINX

or
The Ripper's Tale

A novel by

LAWRENCE DURRELL

faber and faber
LONDON · BOSTON

First published in 1985
by Faber and Faber Limited
3 Queen Square London WC1N 3AU
This paperback edition first published in 1986
Set by Speedspools Edinburgh

Printed in Great Britain by
Richard Clay (The Chaucer Press) Ltd Bungay Suffolk
All rights reserved

British Library Cataloguing in Publication Data

Durrell, Lawrence
Quinx, or, The Ripper's Tale
I. Title
823'.912[F]   PR6007.U76
ISBN 0-571-13954-X

inscribed to Stela
A. Ghetie

. . . must itself create the taste by which it is to be judged . . .
Wordsworth *dixit*

Contents

ONE

Provence Anew

THE TRAIN BORE THEM ONWARDS AND DOWNWARDS through the sluices and barrages which contained the exuberance of the Rhône, across the drowsy plain, towards the City of the Popes, where now in a frail spring sunshine the pigeons fluttered like confetti and the belfries purged their guilt in the twanging of holy bells. Skies of old rose and madder, flowering Judas and fuchsia, mulberry and the wise grey olives after Valence.

They were met by the long-lost children they called "the Ogres" accompanied by the faithful Drexel. They had come to carry out the long-promised plan of retirement to the remote chateau which the brother and sister had inherited. Here they were to bury themselves in the three-cornered love which had once intrigued Blanford and caused him to try to forge a novel round the notion of this triune love. Alas, it had not come off. The idea, like the reality, had been too gnostic and would, in the reality also, fail. But now they were happy and full of faith, the beautiful ogres. Blan greeted them tenderly.

For their own part they looked rather like the members of a third touring company of a popular play – the two fair women and the boy, Lord Galen, Cade, Sutcliffe, Toby and so on. Be ye members of one another, he thought. If each had a part in the play perhaps they could also be the various actors which, in their sum, made up one whole single personality? The sunshine slumbered among the roses and somewhere a nightingale soliloquised. He had made one gesture which adequately expressed his feeling that this was to be a new beginning to his life. He had thrown away all his notes for the new book, shaking out his briefcase from the window of the train and watching the leaves scatter and drift away down the valley of the Rhône. Like a tree shedding its petals – slips of all colours and sizes. He had decided the night before that if ever he wrote again it would be without premeditation, without notes and plans, but spontaneously as a cicada sings in the summer sunlight. The fat man, his alter ego, watched him as he did so and expressed a certain reserve by shaking his head very doubtfully as he watched the petals floating away in a vast whirl just like the pigeons over the town. It would be like this after the atomic explosion, he was thinking – just clouds of memoranda filling the air – human memoranda. The sum of all their parts whirled in the death-drift of history – motes in a vast sunbeam.

Cade suddenly laughed and struck his thigh with his palm, but he did not share the joke with them. Perhaps it was not a joke?

Sutcliffe said with dismay: "But surely we aren't going to let the ogres re-enact the terrible historic mistake which was the theme of your great epos – the heroic threesome of romance? Come! It didn't work in life any more than it worked in the novel, admit it!" Aubrey did, but with bad grace. "Three into one don't go." Pursued his alter ego: "Though God knows why not – we should ask Constance, for perhaps the old Freudian canon can tell us why. Anyway, if it was good enough for Shakespeare it is good enough for me!"

"What do you mean by that?"

"The Sonnets. The situation outlined in them would have made perhaps his finest play, but he fought shy of it because instinctively he felt that it wouldn't work. We must really try to save the poor ogres from the same fate – not let them come round again on the historic merry-go-round with the hapless Drexel. Save them! History, memory, you promised to avoid all those traps: otherwise you will simply have another addition to the *caveau de famille* of the straight novel and Sylvie will remain forever in the asylum, lying under her tapestry and writing . . ."

"She has been trying to write my book, the one I am just about to begin by marshalling all these disorderly facts into a coherent maze of language where everyone will find his or her place without jostling or hurry. But I realise now that if you don't have the built-in intimations of immanent virtue as described by Epicurus, say, you will end up with an excessive puritan morality, and overcompensate by unscrupulousness, even by sheer bloodlust, marked by sentimentality. At the same time one must tiptoe and with care, one must advance *au pifomètre*, 'by dead reckoning'." It was obvious to both that the sort of book they sought must not repeat the misadventure of Piers and Sylvie for what they wanted to refresh and reanimate was the archaic notion of the couple, the engineers of grace through the act. Actually it had happened, and thanks to Constance, her massage and her physical pleading had suddenly awoken his spine and with it the whole net of ganglia which revived and tonified his copulatory powers. Thaumatology! the death-leaps of the divine orgasm like a salmon: the two-in-one joined by an immense but penetrable amnesia which they could render gradually more and more conscious. To hold it steady to the point of meditation where it is blinding and then slowly melt one into the other with a passion which was all stealth . . . Who abdicates in love wins all! "The Garden of the Hesperides" is within the reach of such . . . The kiss is the pure copula of the vast shared thought. "I love you!" he said with amazement, with real amazement.

"Christ!" he said. "Thanks to you I have come awake for the first time. The horrible sleeping dummy awakens!

Lady Utterly, fancy seeing you! What brings you here?" She settled more closely into the crook of his arm, but did not speak. She knew that the information she had passed on came from her dead lover, Affad. He had always said: "What is too finely explained becomes inoperative, dead, incapable of realisation. Never talk about love unless you are looking elsewhere when you do. Otherwise the self-defeating pillow-music will lead you astray." Blanford was saying: "Darling, you will be able to exhibit me in a glass case outside your consulting-room as 'The man who came back from the dead – the ape erect!' " Ah! but *she* knew that science is not interested in happy endings – that is the privilege of art!

As Sutcliffe used to hum:

> *What he believed in cannot be expressed,*
> *That's why his ideas seem partly undressed*

When insight hardens into dogma it goes dead, so they kept everything fluid yet kept on praying for more and yet more insight with which to discipline the heart. How dull the old world of "before" seemed now with its inappropriate lusts and dilapidated attachments. In the Camargue on the verandah of their little house they sat in silence watching the night falling and the fireflies twinkling like minds realising themselves briefly, abruptly before disappearing. Meanwhile she was making notes for her psychoanalytic essay on that forgotten novel *Gynacocrasy* the reading of which (it was comically pornographic in the stark naivety of its love scenes) had brought them both so much fun. It had clearly been written by a woman and Constance was setting out to prove the fact (which was nowhere stated) purely by internal evidence of a psychoanalytic-sexual kind. Blanford was amazed when he thought how much she had taught him, even physically. She had learned that the priapic conjunction is a force-harness which builds the field in which the future, as exemplified by the human child, can secure a foothold in reality. Half-joking she could say: "Now you know what you are doing when you couple with me you will never be able to leave me – it would be dangerous for your insight! For your art, the merchandise of breath, *oxygen*! We've done it, darling! The orgasm if shared in this way admits you to the realm between death and rebirth, the workshop of both past and future. To grasp this simultaneity is the key. Meanwhile in between births – the orgasm is a shadow-play of this chrysalis stage – we exist in five-skanda form, aggregates, parcels, lots, congeries. They cohere to form a human being when you come together and create the old force-field quinx, the five-sided being with two arms, two legs and the kundalini as properties!"

"Well," he said somewhat ironically, "in the new age it will be the man who is the Sleeping Beauty and who is kissed awake by the woman! Their paths join and bifurcate at the command of nature. And human truth, damn it, must become coeval with nature's basic nonchalance for the miracle to come about. As if one had to stop caring and start improvising! Of course love can be reduced to a pleasant conviviality but the wavelength or scale is low and it cannot fecundate the heart or the insight. A mere discharge cannot instruct!"

"You need to go away from me for a bit now. Not for too long. But to get your focus right for what you want to start building."

"I know," he said. "I shan't be happy until I have had a real try to make it the way I want – being serious without being grave. (The malevolence of too much goodness is to be feared!) If I could create such an edifice it would point the finger at the notion of discrete identity as being very much in question – 'Be ye members of one another' or 'spare parts', *pièces détachées*!"

"What else?" she said in loving triumph.

"Make a playdoyer for coexisting time-tracks in the human imagination. Deal seriously *at last* with human love which is a yogic thought form, the rudder of the human ship of fools: for hidden in the blissful amnesia we have just shared is the five-sided truth about human personality. Meanwhile the text should show high contrivance as well as utter a plea for bliss as being the object of art. Am I talking rubbish? It's euphoria, then!"

But in fact he was right for the idea of chronology had become disturbed – history was not past but was something which was always just about to happen. It was the part of reality that was *poised*! He would have gone out of his mind with all these intimations of another version of reality but for the indispensable beauty and loneliness of her presence. She had said: "If you want to do good without moralising write a poem", and this is what he began to feel might lie within his powers one day soon!

"You will soon be in a position to write a study of the woman as placebo – the therapy takes place even if she is not a goddess but an ordinary woman!" (Sutcliffe sounded a little jealous, perhaps he was.) She said: "But you are *right*. It's her role. And each orgasm is a dress rehearsal for something deeper, namely death, which becomes more and more explicit until it happens and revives the whole universe in us at a blow. Knowing this you know that everything is to be forgiven, none of our trespasses need be taken too seriously. Fundamentally everyone is panning for gold."

"I hate this kind of moralising," he said, "because it smells of self-righteousness. I want to be bad, just bad. It's also a way of loving – or isn't it? I know you are thinking of the philosopher Daimonax, but was he right when he said that nobody really wanted to be bad? We must ask Sabine."

And fortunately Sabine was there to ask, sitting at the table on the balcony with her eternal spread of cards before her, scrutinising the future. She was smoking a cheroot as she worked – for skrying is hard work. She said: "It's better than that, even, for the whole universe; the whole of process, to the degree that it is natural, becomes pain-free, anxiety-free, stress-free. The lion was made to lie down with the lamb – only anxiety causes fear, causes war. The same with us. Love and lust are forms of spiritual traction which a girl knows instinctively how to handle – the push and pull of sexual and bisexual feeling, the dear old Oedipus group. Unless one grasps this one goes on living with sadness – the horror at the meaninglessness of things keeps on increasing. But reality is really bliss-side-up if we want it so. Constance must purge your nursery desires, evolve your feeling for emptiness, develop the vatic sense, and persuade the heart to become festive!"

"Yes!" said Constance slowly. "And birth is no trauma but an apotheosis: here I part company with my Viennese colleagues for they were born into sin. But in reality one is born into bliss – it is we who cause the trauma with these mad doctrines based on guilt and fear. Pathology begins at home!"

"Instinct has its own logic which we must obey, we can't do otherwise. We must roll with the hunch, so to speak. It is independent of the quantitative method which just brings up samples to analyse, all parts of an incommensurable whole."

It was now that she told them the tale of Julio, the gipsy poet, and the story of his legs. He had been the only child produced by the Mother and nobody knew what his origins were for She had never been seen to "accept" a man in her caravan. It was understood that such a weakness would have in some way qualified her "sight", diminished her powers of prophesy. Julio grew up into a godly magnificence, physically of fine stature, and composed as if he had already lived on earth before. Not to mention *une sexualité à tout va* . . . He made up for his mother's shortcomings and had all the beauties of the

17

tribe in love with him. He became the tribal bard, so to speak, though among gipsies there is no such thing. His compositions were improvised to the guitar but the words were so striking they became popular sayings. He still lives on in quotation, so to speak.

"But it was not only love-making that Julio favoured, he was also an athlete and enjoyed cattle-rustling and cockade-snatching – the variety of bull-fighting favoured by all Provence. He liked the taste of danger in the cockade fight and became a champion – unusual for a gipsy. Then came his downfall." Pain entered Sabine's quiet voice. "He was matched against the famous bull Sanglier who was also a champion, and a fierce combat ensued. Julio almost flew in this battle, and the old bull used every trick in his repertoire, for he was a seasoned defender of the little red cockade. Then came the climax. Julio slipped as he came to the barrier and lost his advantage over the bull. Sanglier bustled him to the barricades and with an experienced maliciousness savaged him. When you are passing in the Camargue and you come across the tomb of this heroic Homeric animal, say a prayer for the ghost of Julio for he had both legs so badly crushed against the barrier that they were forced to amputate them. We thought he would die of misery and physical humiliation but after a period of despair, during which he selected and rejected every form of suicide, he took on a new life. His poetry increased in vigour and gravity. He had asked for his legs back, and these he had beautifully embalmed as an *ex voto* for Saint Sara. They were placed in the grotto with the spring at the Pont-du-Gard and a cult of fertility grew up about them. But this was after his death, for he lived on for a number of years just as a stump of flesh with arms, and strangely enough his success with the women increased rather than diminished. He never wanted for women. It was said that the infertile conceived after a love-bout with Julio. All the sexual power of his lost legs seemed to have entered his member. It grew enormous, he was in permanent erection it seemed. I went to him myself once or twice out of curiosity and he was extraordinary. He seemed to bore to the very heart of the orgasm – the psyche's point of repair, the site of its sexual health. With the missing legs one could see that the spinal column was really a sort of Giant's Causeway towards the yogic self-comprehension – the kundalini, serpent-erect business. Julio had imbibed this from his mother's milk. I myself realised for the first time that sex is not dying, it is coming of age with the freedom of the woman. Its real secrets are as yet only half-fathomed in the West. The mathematics of the sexual act remain obscure. The power of five is really the riddle of the Quinx – solve it if you dare! But the problem of Julio is a very grave political one for us. Unless they are rediscovered and the shrine of Sara given back to us the Tribe can neither march nor procreate!"

"Two down and five across, a ruling passion."
"Tagged by the Greeks as psyche-fed?"
"No. No. Five letters, love. I love you!"
"But psyche-fed no less, for love's the
Four-letter word we most recall with
Never a crossword or dull moment. Two
Across and one up, never a cross word!"

To codify the appetites by yoga – all kisses and sweet stresses, sweet stretches and breathwork, guarding the deep vascularity of muscles and veins. Then meditation, like crossing the dark garden of consciousness shielding a lighted candle which the least puff of wind might extinguish. You protect this small precarious flame, treasuring it in the palm of the hand. So very gradually your meditation affirms and strengthens the flame and you can cross the dark garden with it triumphantly erect – the yoga erection of the adept in Tao is this, no? Yes, in Taoist terms even love is a predicament due to the wrong angle of inclination towards the universe.

He sees no contradiction in contradiction, and to know this is the beginning of a freakish new certainty. His poetry is concerned with the transmission of an inkling, a breath of the supreme intuition which makes you laugh inside forever!

"I am grateful to Egypt – having my back shot to pieces. I might never have bothered with this yoga jape and so missed a deeply transforming experience. A religion which harbours no ifs and buts, not even the shadow of a perhaps. No sweet neurosis this, no mental chloroform pad! Formal logic dissolves and as you orchestrate the body you exchange lard against oxygen. The hunger is not to possess, to own, but to belong."

> Parts and wholes
> Wholes and parts
> Private parts and
> Public holes
> Holy Poles
> Unholy poles
> Wholly wholes.

"If you suffer from a Priapus afflicted by Saturn you will do anything to make ends meet." (Sutcliffe)

He dreamed of something as lovely and deliberate as the kisses of pretty Turkish *hanoums* in their sherbet heaven. An abundance of smiling ticklers, an alphabet of broken sighs, oriental codes of sex. And all he got was that a girl like a pterodactyl silked him off in the bus from Gatwick crying, "Bless Relaxers!" By not minding we gain a little ground.

SUT AND BLAN
SOUL AND BODY = prototypes of love and folly lie there and play with your Vertical Banjo!

Puella lethargica dolorosa! Just kissing you was like a telephone call from God! Why then did you go away and ride to hounds? A non-man is worse than a con-man. He will wither your sense and sap your succulence. "Not to know one's own mind is for a woman the beginning of wisdom!" (Inscription on a Persian pisspot.)

Running along the grey-green river they had seen the famous broken bridge, still pointing its reproachful finger across the water towards the waterless *garrigue*. Neither Blanford nor Sutcliffe could resist the prompting to hum out:

> *Sur le pont d'Avignon*
> *on y pense, on y pense . . .*
> *sur le pont d'Avignon*
> *on y pense, tout en rond!*

"How much longer have we got together?" asked Blanford and his alter ego replied: "One more book, one more river. Then body and soul must end their association. I know. It's too short. It's the only criticism one can make of life. It's too short to learn anything."

"Constance looks ill."

"She will recover. I promise."

> *Rose de la poésie, O belle névrose!*

But even God must be subject to entropy if he exists. Or has he learned to enjoy and use the death-drift from perfection to putridity? Does he live like the Taoist in a perpetual holy irreverence?

make his bed   perhaps some passages in primal scene
take his life   verse? Maybe Sutcliffe would share a

mark his pillow
'absent wife'
darn his heel
smoke his quid
doing all
the other did
hunt the slipper
hunt the soul
Eros teach him
breath control!

Hearts-and-Flowers act with his alter ego?

Scene of the epilepsy, the pearl saliva,
The tongue bitten in half, almost
    swallowed.

"Cybele! What's for dinner?"
"Uterus!" she said.

Carry thy balls high, Coz, *les couilles bien haut! Recuser, accoler, accusez, raccolez!*

When young my member diminished like a candle under her caresses; but age and meditation stiffen resolve and now she knows how to mature and guide the trophy of erectile tissue in order to make it act responsibly. Today I feel I could write cheques with it if necessary. (Sutcliffe)

The old valiant rises and retains its discharge politely like a clergyman at a tea-party, giving infinite service with infinite politeness. But it is entirely in the woman's gift. If she wants she can blow it out like a match! (Blan)

The elephant, if you imbibe him, teaches that art is both therapy and moral construction. Its calibre and relevance may vary. Its arithmetic is hermetic. Something goes into nothing once only. Love!

Ah! But to die of sincere haemorrhoids, or by inhaling a banana, or *d'une obésité succulente* – that would be worth-while, artistically. And pray, why not an aberrant prose style to echo the discordance at the heart of all nature? Shackle verbs, give nouns wings, disburse the seven-pronged adjective. Divulge!

Often when they had drunk too much they would have the illusion that it might still be possible to get to the bottom of things. Dialogues like:

BLAN: What would you do if someone said you were not true to life? Eh? Reveal!

SUT: I would be vastly put out. I would sulk.

BLAN: You see, for us in the cinema age reality is recognisable and identifiable only at twenty-eight frames a second. But undercrank and the image goes out of true and becomes aberrant, that of a paranormal person, schizo or parano, whichever you wish.

SUT: Is that the complaint? Not true to life, they say? So there is such a thing to compare me with? I am undercranked and feverish? So this is what mere Relativity has done for us? Catapulted us into the Provisional, with reality as a shadow-world?

BLAN: When I asked Einstein about you, about how much reality I could accord you, he said: "You mean that pink chap who looks like a pig? Tell him from me that man only has a *tendency* towards existing. I can't go any further towards unqualified certainty about his actually being: short of a telex from God, that is!"

SUT: What a dilemma! I am simply symbolic you might say. Symbolic merely, like a teddy bear full of caviar? The people who say this seem unaware that they only camp temporally in their body as in a chrysalis. Then pouf! a moth dedicated to eating cloth. One day I shall acquire a meaning. As in the average novel, "A careful analysis of Nothing reveals that . . . Ambulances bleating for blood all night, flesh and blood. Who can sleep?"

BLAN: Wake then and write our book – a new Ulysses dying of a liturgical elephantiasis. Or dream of a girl on long thirsty legs but as shy as glue. Art has a stance but no specific creed.

SUT: It could borrow one if need be. A smother of girls would be better. You see, we only live in the instant between inhalation and ex-. This point in yoga time is the only history. But suppose we refine and purge and strengthen this small glimpse of truthful time, why, we would redeem eternity, the heraldic vision, the panoramic insight!

BLAN: Oh well, so what then?

SUT: You have me there. What then indeed?

BLAN: Philosophâtre or Psycholope
Come and join the Bank of Hope
Like royal swans in helpless rut
Or dirty ducks in hopeless goose
Wake Psyche from her trance
Lest she should die of self-abuse
And take a lesson from the dead
For history is a running noose.

SUT: So I really mean nothing? Symbol without translation?

BLAN: All symbols start like that. Happily meaning has a tendency to accrete in time around an enigma. I don't know why. As if nature could not rest without offering a gloss. In poetry the obscure becomes slowly invested with meaning as if by natural law. The big enigmas of art, simply by dint of continuing to exist, finally accumulate their own explanations by the force of critical projection. Mozart's Commendatore, for example, is regarded as so mysterious, yet because he still lives, thanks to the electric charge conferred on him by his maker, he becomes daily more significant. One day soon the "meaning" will burst upon us.

SUT: Agreed. But this information is available to the woman from the resources of her female intuition. It may remain unformulated but somewhere she knows that she is the custodian of his poetry, her role is to recognise and release the rare moth which can be housed in the most loathsome caterpillar's form. The act of sex bursts through the container of the flesh in an act of recognition. Presto! Liberation of poet-moth!

BLAN: Wow!

SUT: As you say, wow!

BLAN: *Touche-partout, couche-partout,*
Bon à rien, prêt à tout.

What about love?

A girl in grey with one dark note,
Pitched somewhere between fox and dove,
Soft as the driven television must
Like all our lovers come to dust.

Think of others who have passed this way. Lust for a comprehensive vision which death repays in dust. Nicholas De S. Better to become a best seller and spend your life fingering the moister parts of the Goddess of Pelf! E.A.P. his brain burst on the job. The perilous ascension of artistic ichor in the bloodstream, the panoramic vision – it was too much for him. It swallowed him. He was dragged by the hair into the cave of the oceanic consciousness, the Grendel's cave of art's origins; drink drank him.

(Sutcliffe pours out a drink.)

And K? As his mind ran down he grew more yellow and wasted, blooming now like a waxlight, a Jewish taper burning inside a coffin. His hands grew covered with warts which suppurated. Staring into the maw of the Jewish superego.

Tolle lege, tolle lege. Voices that St Augustine heard, of children in some forsaken garden singing for the birthday of an angel. The imperative of the poet. Hush, can you hear them?

The doomboat of our culture filling up, the ship of fools. But it only looks like that. Actually if you believe, as I do, that all people are slowly becoming the same person, and that all countries are merging into one country, one world, you will be bound to see all these so-called characters as illustrations of a trend. They may be studied through their weaknesses of which the greatest and most revealing is their disposition to love and produce copies in flesh of their psychic needs. Do you see?

B. thinks: Death seems various and quite particular because our friends die in scattered fashion, one by one, slipping out of the décor and leaving holes in it. But as a principle it is as universal as all becoming is – *semper ubique*, old boy – though the effect is slow-motion. The ship shakes itself and settles with a shiver before she dives. Experienced sailors notice the premonitory quiver and cry, "She's settling!" long before the cry goes up, "There she goes!" The spring will seem endless once back in Avignon. Constance: I love you and I want to die.

Sutcliffe had a friend who died in action but continued his erection into *rigor mortis*. This was quite a sight and caused an admiring crowd of nurses who had been on short commons for some time and were anxious for novelties. A thing like this mauve member could satisfy an army of them, they thought, and kept coming back to look and exult. But it faded with the sunset when they came to lay him out.

Blan said grumpily: "But we shall end like some old bow-wow and toddle off to Doggy Heaven in Disneyland or Forest Lawns where telegrams are delivered to Little Fido

when he has crossed the Styx. Charon delivers them without
a word, pocketing the dollar with a grin as he rows away.

> To each his tuffet
> And so some Miss Muffet.
> (Many are called but most are frigid.
> Some need theosophy to keep them rigid.)
>
> Deep in its death-muse Europe lay.
> Boys and girls come out to play.
>
> *Fruit de mer* beyond compare,
> Suck a sweeter if you dare.
>
> Ashes to ashes, lust to lust,
> Their married bliss a certain must.
>
> He storied urn, she animated bust.

The day when Aristotle decided (*malgré lui*) that the
reign of the magician-shaman was over (Empedocles), was
the soul's D-Day. The paths of the mind had become over-
grown. From that moment the hunt for the measurable
certainties was on. Death became a constant, the ego was
born. Monsieur came down to preside over the human
condition:

> To kill to eat was nature's earlier law.
> To kill to kill created a furore.
> Such abstract murder could not come amiss
> So Christians sublimated with The Kiss
> And drunk on blood they broke the body's bread
> To make a cold collation for the dead!

Listen, nothing that SUT has to say about BLAN should
be taken too seriously, for he is only a creation of the latter,

his Tu Quoque, existing by proxy. Is BLAN then King? Yes, in a way, but his powers are somewhat diminished, he can't see very far, whereas SUT is the third eye, so to speak. His belly-button pierces the future, the all-seeing eye of time. Is this what has poisoned the life of the solitary author as he files his nails and watches the snow falling eternally over Blandshire? Why the devil had he chosen a profession which involved him in the manufacture of these paper artefacts – characters which drained him of so much life that he often felt quite one-dimensional, himself equally a fiction of his fictions? Eh? After the publication of SUT's autobiography, in which he figured, fame was not long in coming, though both men had begun to feel wholly posthumous. But SUT became slowly so popular that he became detached like a retina, or else loosed like a soap-bubble to float about in the public consciousness like a sort of myth. He had made the English language, had the old Ripper, while Blanford had hardly made *Who's Who*.

"*O Anax* – the Big Boss, whose shrine is at Delphi, neither hides nor reveals, but simply signifies or hints!"

Similarly all writers are the same one, Blake scribbles Nietzsche's notes on the same experience . . . Trickling through the great dam of the human sensibility, charting the depths and the shallows. Sometimes imperfect texts give off the authentic radium, like the shattered lines of Heraclitus, O Skotinos, the Darkling One! It still vibrates in the mind like a drum-beat.

Rozanov whose originality lay in his truth, capturing thought just as it was about to burst like a bubble upon the surface of human consciousness, of *meaning*. Neither good nor bad, simply what is. Just inkling. A highly pathological and precarious art flowed from this practice in Western terms: in Eastern terms he was writing entirely in *koans*, not in

epigrams. To be thought of as the start of a religious quest –
doubt, anxiety, stress. The soul's traction!

SUT receives a postcard from Toby who is lecturing in
Sweden: "Come north at once! The Swedes are quite
marvellous. They have souls like soft buttocks and buttocks
like hard soles."

He has caused considerable annoyance by describing the
nouveau roman, of which they stand in superstitious awe as:
"*Les abats surgelés des écrivains qui refusent toute jouissance.*"

In the Paris *métro* he caught sight of the new woman we
have all been on edge to meet – the Rosetta Stone, fresh from
the USA. "She wore an inflatable air jacket stolen from Air
France. Trousers lined with newspaper – the *Tribune*. She
carried a traffic sign torn living from the landscape around
Fifth and Sixth, reading YIELD. She sucked her thumb when
doing nothing – nails bitten down to the quick. And twitching
with hemp smoke. A choice young cliterocrat."

The sperm does not age as man himself does. Even an
old man can make a young baby.

> Envenomed by solitude and vanity,
> Created sound and yet forbidden sanity.

SUT: (To his shaving mirror) "Ah! the dear old face,
like a bony housing for the critical motor, eyes, nose, mouth,
cruel uncial smiles, eyebrows cautious circumflex. Toughened
by weather, roughened by thought, weathered by sighs so
dearly bought. Needs repainting. The eyes shouting 'Help!'
The eyes pleading diminished responsibility."

By hoping, wishing and foreseeing we are doing something contrary to nature. *Cogito* is okay but *spero* makes man
out of the featureless animal of Aristotle: gone astray in the
forebrain.

SUT: "*La femme en soi si récherchée par l'âme. La femme en soie, brave dame.*

> *Boule Quies d'aramanthe et camfre*
> *Une veuve de Cigue*
> *Trinquer avec la mort!*
> *Cliquot Cliquot Cliquot*
>> *Trinc trinc*
>> *La Veuve Cliquot!*"

BLAN: "In the account I propose to give of your marriage I propose to heighten the colour in the interest of my fiction with additions gleaned from Constance who talked about it with sympathy and sorrow. Explaining with all the vivacity of my prose style how everything had been complicated and poisoned beyond endurance by this unlucky marriage to a captious little queen of the greatest charm and style who disguised her proclivities very cleverly, by sleeping with many men openly, and as many women secretly. It was easy, really, for you were a highly intelligent man – that is to say, a fool!"

SUT: "I was inexperienced, I suppose, and of course when one falls in love one is simply 'imprinted' by the projection of one's desire, like a duckling falling in love with its keeper's shoe. Yet I should have known. Those dry airless kisses tasting of straw were puzzling, the caresses of the mantis. Then the dry marsupial pocket of the rarely used vagina should have drawn attention to the enormous and beautiful clitoris. She was a trifle painful to penetrate but in every other respect normal and valiant. It took some time to find out that she shammed her orgasms, or else (to judge by the few involuntary expressions that escaped her lips) thought of someone else while doing. She had avoided marriage all these years, why had she turned aside for me?"

BLAN: "I don't know. Perhaps the male gender of the tribe have a weakness for young married women and the ring excites them for they are at one and the same time both cheating and aping the man. Excalibur! How joyfully they humiliate hubby and betray him! Suddenly the whole business became clear to him, the meaning of that large circle of female friends, all very feminine and unsatisfied (if one were to believe them) in their married lives. As she said, they had 'thrown themselves away' on Tom, Dick and Harry. Then of course the conventions aided things. Nobody bothers about women kissing and hugging each other, a little conventional 'mothering' is quite in order, or trotting off to the powder room together while the husbands solemnly suck their pipes and talk about holy orders!"

She was no larger than a pinch of snuff but she packed some sneeze! *Une belle descente de lit.*

S: God, what dreadful French!

B: I know. Showing off again. Go on.

Well, he found himself gradually propelled into a sort of travesty of the female role. He did the washing up and stayed behind to watch the dinner cook while she hopped off with a friend to have her horoscope cast by another friend. The telephone went all the time with a susurrus of private jokes and social plans. He opened a private letter one day in error, having mistaken the handwriting (he would never have dared nor wished to spy on her) and at once interpreted all these ambiguities correctly. Thought suddenly of the so called "masculine protest" – the tiny moustache which was so painfully removed by wax depilatory or dabbed with peroxide. The green ink, and the wearing of charms and necklaces and *one earring*!

Amo, amas, amat. Je brûle, chérie, comme une chapelle ardente! Baise-moi! Self-righteousness, hunger for propitiation, vainglory, sanctimoniousness – Sutcliffe: "At your service, old man: at your mercy."

I am adding an anecdote from someone else – Fatima,

to be precise. "Let's make love, it will be good for each other's French." It was not very satisfactory, she had all the desperation of a woman who knows she is too fat. But after all she was game and later she cried with a mixture of vexation and stark pleasure. What did I like in her? She was lush with worldliness and had a peach-vulgar face. But the smell of her thighs was rich with an instinctual sweat hinting of musk; wherever you licked her skin was dewy as a rose. I licked and licked like a *drogué en état de manque!* – her own expression.

Toby, regarding himself in his shaving mirror, exclaims: "Mean-spirited gnome! If it were not for your beauty I would leave you!" His ad is still going in the *Trib*. It runs: "Elderly vampire (references) living in kind of doomed old mansion near Avignon seeks rational diversions."

He also said: "Other men drink to forget but I drink to remember!"

The poetic substance detached from the narrative line, the sullen monorail of story and person. Rather to leave the undeveloped germs of anecdote to dissolve in the mind. Like the accident, the death in a snowdrift near Zagreb. The huge car buried in a snowy mountain. She was in full evening dress with her fur cape, and the little cat Smoke asleep in her sleeve. The headlights made a blaze of crystal so it seemed the snow was lit from within. But they forgot to turn the heaters off. A white Mercedes with buried lights. Why go on? They suffocated slowly while waiting for help which could not reach them much before dawn. Only Smoke remained. Her loud purring seemed to fill the car.

A letter from faraway London. Grey skies. Pissing in the bull's eye of a Twyford's "Adamant". BLAN was forced to write on a postcard: "Be warned that daydreaming is not meditating. Inquisitiveness is not curiosity. Beware of the brass rubbings of a demon culture. Identikit husbands and wives!"

Eclair, who wrote the review, was a generous old French pedal, tightwad like most, burning with a hard bumlike flame. He wrote about the poet as if he were a sort of stair carpet wreathed in Scotch mist. He curled his hair with hot-smelling tongs and ate much convincing garlic with his choice high-flown game. Yet he understood all, revealed all! It was uncanny. "A good artist has every reason to enjoy his approaching death – his life would have proved to be a scandal of inattention otherwise!"

B: Where do people end? Where do their imaginations begin? I have been a sleepwalker in literature. My books have happened to me *en route*. I am at a loss to account for them, to ascribe any special value to them. Perhaps they may be marvellous to other sleepwalkers, serving as maps? Who can tell? Socially I am a fig-eater. I have always believed in myself – *credo quia absurdam*! Given to baroque turns of speech, in writing I wished to substitute intricacy for podge.

> Go and catch a falling whore,
> That's what she is waiting for.
> Ah! pretty frustrate pray unlatch
> And bid poor Jenkins down the hatch.
> A rose by any other name
> Would smell as good where'er it came.
> Great Lover, that involuntary clown
> Will always having his trousers falling down.
> To scrape a furtive living from the arts
> And keep intact his shrinking private parts . . .

The lover now belongs to an endangered species for science threatens him with extinction. Maybe Stekel will have the last word on your marriage after all: "It is evident that a sadistic atmosphere was cultivated in this marriage. The fact that both parties were homosexual led to a peculiar sort of inversion. He played with the wife the role of a woman who has intercourse with a woman, and she that of a man having intercourse with a man. This bound them together. Those movements which excited him at coitus resembled the convulsive twitching of death. And surprisingly, in contrast to his fantasies of violence he was aware that potency disappeared if that woman moved. She must lie still, grow pale, resemble as much as possible a corpse. Thus he was aroused sadistically and restored to full potency."

For some reason this irritated Sutcliffe who said: "I often see us as a couple of old whores, dead drunk, who toddle off into the night towards Marble Arch, having emptied their bladders accidentally into each other's handbag."

It was obvious that in common with most of us they were hunting a spontaneity which had once been innate, given, and to which the key had been mislaid.

Though spring was here the station of Avignon was a draughty place to argue about who was going to stay where. Finally the main party decided to stay with Lord Galen whose establishment was the most comfortable until such time as the house belonging to Constance in Tubain was ready to receive them. This would give them a valuable respite of a few days to organise the plumbing and painting which was undoubtedly quite necessary after years of neglect. It was astonishing even that the edifice remained watertight and with a solid roof after so many war years. But surely all this could be put right for a summer; in a vague way the notion recaptured some of the *élan* of that earlier holiday – situated in prehistory it would seem now – when they had all been young. Before the War?

The kiss of Judas – the poisoned arrow of our history became something one could learn for kitchen consumption. Seen from the point of view of the City of the Popes it signified the truth of the matter – namely, that our whole civilisation could be seen as a tremendous psychic mishap. The baritone pigeons crooning among the tintinabulous belfries calling the faithful to prayer which had become a mere expedient, not a way of breathing.

"I am writing a defence of Inklings."

going	"Inklings of what?"	dying
going	"Of the absolute, silly."	dying
gone	"And what, pray, may that be?"	dead
	"An inkling."	

SUT said: "I have taken another and less uncommon path. Ever since I founded my group, called Mercy-Fucking for the Hard-Pressed, I have never wanted for clients. The robot did it all."

Lord Galen, who had come silently into the room in order to bid them to dinner in the grange, pricked up his ears and said: "Did I hear the word robot? Why, you take the words out of my mouth. As you know I have great post-war plans for a rational deployment of my capital in several ways. One of them is going to be in marital aids. There will be a great need for marital aids. I am trying to arrange for some to be blessed by the Pope as part of the promotional campaign. The chances seem promising at the moment."

The two men, if that is what one can call them, congratulated him with unfeigned affection and followed him down to the vast kitchens where trestle tables had been laid out for them and the vivid odours of roast pork and ginger flew about like doves of promise. Of course there was constraint – Constance with her silent companion! The little boy had found the two daughters of the caretakers and sat between them happily. The rest disposed themselves around unfinished

conversations and fell to work, served by the old farm woman
and her youthful niece.

How Blanford with his shyness and pain over Constance
irritated the lady as he eyed her; she glared down at her hands,
resenting his air of inescapable chasteness – the despair of a
Prometheus chained to the bleak rock of his moral virginity.
She hated him! What a self-satisfied little prig!

"My yoga teacher told me that one of the great problems
of the hermetic schools was to prevent the lama turning into
a robot, to prevent him falling asleep at his loom. Don't you
think that is a fair comment on Lord Galen's marital aids?
After all, a simple kiss describes a trajectory through the
human consciousness, for it raises the blood heat and adds to
secretions like sugar and insulin. You may be sure that Judas
knew that."

"Pity you emptied out all those notes over the valley.
You will feel the need of them."

"I have them all here, night and day." He tapped his
forehead. "You will notice them coming up in my conversation because they represented my most intimate obsessions,
problems I could not solve; and without a solution I could not
advance in my heart. For instance, problems of form and style
essential to my new book. I was much encouraged by the
courage shown by Rozanov, and also by the jumpy hysterical
jottings of Stendhal in his *Souvenirs Intimes* – half-intelligible
as many were. They carried his authentic quirk, unmistakable
turn of speech. They helped me in my search for a form. I said
to myself that one does not look for great truths in a panto-
mime, but how refreshing if you found some in this form,
no?"

"I am a modern man," said SUT, "and I think men
wonderful in principle; but of all men the most wonderful
seems to be me. I am sublime. Nature exhausted Herself in

creating me. Other men – well, how easy to see that she ran out of ideas. They are tadpoles. Do you tell me that your yoga can cure such a conviction?"

"Yes. As it cured my back pains. Relief of stress caused by pressure of an unduly swollen ego. It could lead to trouble in the long run."

"But you are talking as if I am real. Here I have been feeling so diaphanous and now you tell me I am tangible."

"As tangible as a marker in a hymn book; but you cannot sing any of the psalms, my boy.

> *The pathos of metaphor will spell*
> *The secrets of your wishing well,*
> *Brainless as odalisques must be –*
> *The difference twixt thee and me.*
> *To catch a wind, put out a sail.*
> *To catch a mind, put out a soul."*

The wine, a wonderful Fitou, was taking its toll and enlivening the talk. They found themselves liking each other's company more than they had realised; only Constance and her companion lived in a cage of silence and ate with lowered heads. Lord Galen was joyful in his brainless way and Cade watched them all from under his drawn brows, like a mouse from its hole in the infinite.

And that beautiful profligate, the choice companion of Constance, what of her? Sometimes with a hanging head she wept silently from pure joy at her lot, at her luck. Blanford watched her superstitiously and with unwilling sympathy. She wore vast golden sashes to match torrential golden hair and blue eyes full of humour; their constant gaze made them seem like the riding lights of an anchored yacht. Lips uncials of sweet compliance. But she was never quite present, always listening to the inward monitor of a restless mind at odds with itself. Yet watching her and remembering some of the things she had written in the manuscripts which Constance had shown him he realised with envy the truth of her beauty and her genius. Softly he repeated to his own mind, "I dream of writing of an unbearable felicity. I want to saturate my text with my teleological distress yet guard its slapstick holiness as something precious. To pierce the lethargy, indolence and distress of my soul. But the boredom of knowing the truth about things is killing me – the overturned cradle! You see, time, which we all believe in, becomes solid if it persists long enough. Time becomes *mass* in mathematics. For everything is obstinately and deliberately turning into its opposite. That is the nature of process when you get behind the law of cosmic inertia. The universe simply does the *next thing*; it has no programme, does not predict, knows not where it is going. A perpetual spontaneity rules!" He was jealous of Sylvie. She had no right to know so much.

No wonder Constance had succumbed to the appeals of such a heart. And the epigraph she had chosen was apt for her state – the exclamation of Laforgue: "*Je m'ennuie natale!*" Yet he told himself: "I did not expect to be wholly original; secretly I did not think I was really in the Grand Class. But I decided to strive for the heights and at least make myself wholly contemporary, absorbing all the fads and poisons and truths of the age, fully aware of the danger of overturning my applecart by caring too deeply. Yet simply to go on without achieving anything of note – the idea was unbearable. And end up in old age ravaged by the terrible priapism of the very old – ineffectual, burning, solitary: and powerless against the pangs of diurnal lust. Not that!"

Depth of focus is everything in passion as in prose. No more, please God, of those big-paunched invertebrate novels of yore, full of rose-water. An attitude to love which has taken the tang out of tupping. Prose style known to the French as *genre constation de gendarme*.

Reality which seems completely merciless is completely just, being neither for nor against. Sometimes he caught sight of her profile, or the head half-turned towards the source of light. How munificent her deep gloating regard, the sumptuous swarthiness. (The dead are heaped around us in a state of failure.) The single imperative of the artist (everyman) is *bricoler dans l'immédiat, c'est tout*! Reduce the work load of the heart, the tourist heart. Sutcliffe must have been following his thought for he said now: "Vulgarity in love is distressing, and for those who care about it, how vulgar Ovid is! He would work in advertising today, a laureate of Madison Avenue. Propertius, Catullus, *autre chose*." He raised a skinful of wine to his mouth and drank. "Uncanny stuff, wine!" he said, putting down his glass. "I prefer girls of a territorial vastness whose centres of gravity are tellurian tits." Blanford disagreed as he watched the other. With her long white neck she looked like a lily in tears.

Someone commented upon the vastness of Toby's helping whereupon he said huffily: "I have signed no contract with the Holy Ghost to abstain from pork in Lent."

The mansion of Lord Galen had been built in the grounds of an ancient tumbledown *mas*, the manor house of the usual Provençal style of which little remained except several vast granges or outhouses which had been turned into impromptu lodgings against the refurbishing of the newer (and rather hideous in a suburban way) houses. During the harvest and in winter the two further ones were crammed with agricultural machinery like tractors and harrows and combine harvesters. But the one in which they sat down for meals had normally been reserved as a workshop and garage for sick machinery. Exposed on the wall of this rustic dining room was a relic of this mechanical past which had been left behind as a wall decoration. It had great charm because it was clearly an explanatory poster which postdated the invention of the petrol engine by at most ten years. A famous make of automobile offered it to their clients as something which should be on every garage wall where the mechanic could consult it. It was a detailed diagram of a petrol engine extended and exploded so that its parts could be studied separately and their functioning grasped. Each member floated in the air separately, so to speak. This poster formed the backcloth against which Blanford and Sutcliffe sat, and Constance looking over their shoulders studied it with all the medical attention it merited – in the light of her avocation, so to speak. It was an embryology of the petrol engine – the foetal body with all its crude analogies to the human – arms, legs, as wheels, the vertebral column of the human spine. Sump, clutch, cloaca maxima lungs, guts . . .

Some of this thinking was of course Blanford's when he mounted his hobby horse about the flight of the ego to the West. Indeed she could hear his voice parodying her reflections. "Suddenly the human will metastasised, the ego broke loose, took wing in a desire not to conform to nature but to dominate it! A momentous moment, as when Aristotle put the skids under the shaman Empedocles and intellectually fathered Alexander the Great, whose tutor he was! Mind you, the alchemists of old must have known where this prodigious swerve of the human consciousness would lead, this obsession to hunt for the sweetness of traction. As you know, Tibet refused even the wheel – as if to hold up the business as much as possible. Obviously an ego cult fathered upon a driven wheel promised a total drunkenness – a fly-culture over which Mephisto would preside! Yet how irresistibly poetical the quest and how beautiful this racing human diagram in stressed steel, driven by a spark, breath, the cylinder-lungs, the oxygen burning, and the exudation of the waste in calx or smoke through an almost human anus. A fire-chariot woven out of mental stress and the greed of narcissism, self-love, vainglory. It has brought us the unbearable loneliness of speed, of travel, and lastly to the orgasm of flight. As you say, by their fruits shall ye know them. It has brought no peace while a displaced alchemical thirst for gold has attracted the most insecure, the Jews, and has brought us Lord Galen and the World Bank and the Marxist theory of value . . ."

Then he would be visited by a gust of despair and add, characteristically: "O dear! I shall probably end in the condemned cell of some monastery counting the moons of Jupiter for my sins and manicuring my reputation by sonnets." But the diagram would haunt her so that sometimes she was to dream of it, confusing it with an illustration from a medical work on embryology with diagrams of the foetus at various stages of growth, its detached parts all free-floating on the page. Yet her heart applauded him when he added: "But I deplore those who want to make a funk hole or a weeping wall out of the Vedanta, however despicable our present state and however desirable it is that we change our direction before it is too late. Yet destiny is destiny, and ours must work itself out in a Western way, carrying us all with it. Perhaps we could persuade the will to stop clutching; perhaps not. Personally I see no hope, yet I draw my optimism from seeing no grounds for it. I believe in a few things still. You are one."

She had never replied to this but just walked out of the room; but she had tears in her eyes and he noticed this and his heart stirred with conflicting confusions.

But the gruff comment of Sutcliffe was also apposite to the matter. "Crude antithetical thinking", he said, "is the mark of the second-rate mind. It would be fatal to behave as if we had something special to expiate – that would be mere pretension. If you had ever seen a Kashmiri merchant or a Bengali *bunia* or a Hindu business man you would realise that the West has no monopoly in materialism and ego-worship. So there!"

It was true, of course, and Blanford knew it in his heart of minds. His version was too pat. He put aside the latter for the moment. There were more important things afoot. He managed to get the girl aside the next day while Sylvie was having her siesta, a chemical sleep, to say: "You have been up to Tu Duc, and yet you have said nothing about it. I don't even know if it's still standing. I hardly dare to ask." She flushed, overwhelmed by a sudden pudicity. She realised that the whole matter of Sylvie's presence had begun to overcloud the question of them all returning to the *status quo ante*: could he bear to live with her under the same roof? It was unpardonable, what she had forced upon him, and she knew it. Suddenly contrite, she took his arm with all the old affection and said, "Darling Aubrey, yes, it's all there and still in good repair thanks to the new couple Blaise left behind when they went north to a better job with less work. It is all as it was."

Aubrey gazed at her curiously and almost tenderly. "And is It still there – you know what I mean?" Yes, she knew; he meant the old motheaten sofa of Freud, the analytic couch which Sutcliffe had rescued from Vienna a thousand years ago. "Yes, very much so! There is one little mousehole where the stuffing threatens to come out, but I can easily darn it." There was a long silence and then came the question she had been expecting and somewhat dreading. "Are we all going to live together, and if so how?" She herself felt somewhat reluctant to answer it immediately, abruptly, without a preamble of excuse – there had been so much suppressed emotion in his voice. "I thought of giving her Livia's room for the moment. She seems to have fallen in love with it; and she has asked if she might have the couch in it, now she knows its history. She seems to have fallen in love with that too. Aubrey, these are stabilising factors, I am sure you will understand and help. Please say you will."

He gazed at her and nodded slowly. "I shall have to see if I can stand life with you – it's provisional for the moment. But, darling, I can't take up any definite position, I love you too much for that. But the whole thing has been such a shock. And I suppose Cade will have Sam's old room?" She nodded: "If you wish."

"Galen won't want to let us go; he simply has to be surrounded by people or he gets alarmed and lonely!"

"I know. But soon he will have Felix and the Prince to compensate for us. Aubrey, I hope you can face it and be patient." He said, "So do I!" but his tone carried little conviction; nor was there really any alternative, for he was not rich enough to make other arrangements. In his inner mind he swore and ranted at this turn of fate: all the more painful in that she had elected to undertake his treatment, including massage and yoga and electrotherapy. They sat in helpless frustrated silence for a while, staring at each other. She wondered whether or not to carry the story forward and tell him more about this dramatically unreal attachment which had come as much of a surprise to her as to anyone else. But she hesitated. The dilemma was even graver than superficial appearances suggested – professional considerations were inextricably mixed in with them. So it was perhaps inevitable that she should direct her steps towards the lunatic asylum at Montfavet where so much had come to pass during the war years and where her friend Jourdain the doctor still reigned. She had phoned to say she was coming, and it was with smiling deference to her (for he had always loved her but been too shy (unusual in a Frenchman) to tell her so) that he sported his ancient college blazer to remind the world that he was also an MD Edinburgh. Nor was there any insincerity in his exclamation of delight at finding her younger and more beautiful than ever. "Flatterer!" she said, but he shook his head, and then pointed to his own greying hair. Yes, he had aged quite a bit, and was much thinner than when she had last seen him. "Sit down, tell me everything that has happened since last I saw you," he said. And then, realising how impossible a task that would be, added, smiling, "Preferably in one word!" This fell most aptly; she was able to echo his smiling and relaxed mood though what she said was actually laden with sorrow. "That I can," she said, "and the word is . . . Sylvie. I have committed a fearful mistake, and a professional misdemeanour of size. I am in a fix. I want your advice, I need it!"

"Where is she?" he said. "With you?"

"Yes. But as lover, not patient." The sob in her voice startled him and he leaned forward to take her hands as he stared into her eyes with astonishment and commiseration. He whistled softly. "But after all the precautions? India? Really, I thought . . ." She shook her head and said, "I must explain it all in order – even though I can't excuse this terrible and quite astonishing aberration. Where to begin, though?"

Where indeed?

How humiliating too after so many years to come back here, not for treatment, but for moral advice – to what Schwartz always called the "dingy *baisodrome* of French psychiatry"! Talk of being made to swallow toads! She laughed ruefully. "But what went wrong?" he said, his amazement quite unabated. "After all, when first the situation developed we all behaved with impeccable professional zeal. You were alleged to have gone to India and I took your place. Then she was transferred by you to Geneva and the care of Schwarz. Then what?"

"It worked reasonably well until the day when Schwartz elected to commit suicide and I had to take over his dossier in default of anyone better. I returned from India, so to speak, and came once more face to face with her. I experienced the most dramatic and irresistible countertransfer you can think of. The base must have been some slumbering and neglected homosexual predisposition, but the motor which set it off was, inexplicably enough, the death of Schwartz, who was a dear and long-time friend and colleague though nothing more. Inexplicable! Inexplicable!"

"Love is!" said Jourdain, ruefully gazing at her down-cast blonde head and lowered eyes so full of chagrin. "It wasn't love but infatuation – though what matter our silly qualifications? It's just because I feel guilty and ashamed – I should never have succumbed, yet I did."

"And now?"

"But there is worse to come," she said, "for another strange experience awaited me. I had been locked into this experience with such a savage intensity that I think I must have been a little bit out of my mind. I could not breathe without her, could not sleep, read, work . . . Yes, but all this (I see the despairing faces of my friends) – all this melted like an icecap just when we crossed over the border into France. It was as if I had crossed into a territory policed by the part of myself which still belonged to Sam – an older self, apparently long since dead and done with. But no. I realised with a sudden jolt that I was not a homosexual at all but a woman – a man's woman. And the shock spread right through my nervous system so that I think that for a brief moment I may well have passed out. I loved just as intensely, but as a friend; the whole of the sexual component, as uncle Freud would so chastely say, flew out of the window. I was suddenly completely anaesthetic to feminine caresses. They were so light, so insubstantial, trivial as feathers. I suddenly knew I belonged to the hairy race of men. But there, Aubrey has always said that I am a bit of a slowcoach and am afraid to make love without a *garde-feu*. But do you see my dilemma now? O God!" She was pale with fury.

"But why did you come back here?" he asked.

"I had several reasons, among them some quite un-finished business with myself – I wanted to find out a little more about my sister Livia, her death and so on. Then I felt in a vague sort of way that psychologically it might be good to move her back into an old context which must certainly be familiar – though I haven't yet dared to bring her back here to see you. Yet she knows I am here, and even hesitated about sending you a message, so that she still remembers you . . . But now it's me who is in a mess, for I simply do not dare to tell her about my state of mind. I have to sham an affection which I no longer feel for fear of upsetting the pre-carious applecart of her mind again! It would be ridiculous if it were not both painful and humiliating. You see, she is valuable, valuable to us all, her talent, her genius even. We haven't a right to put that at risk – or at least I don't dare. On the other hand I feel like a suburban housewife who has fallen in love with the milk roundsman but does not dare to risk being divorced for it! Sutcliffe was right to laugh when I told him; instead of sympathy he said, 'I think your policemen are simply wonderful!' Like the historic American in London. I suppose he was right."

"But I don't see how your *ménage* is going to work out without stress at some point."

"I know."

"*Ménage* or *manège*! That is the question."

"Help!"

"How can I? You must live it out."

"I know." She stood up, glancing at her watch. "I must go back. But you see? Already I feel better for having ventilated the matter, even though I knew no solution would be forthcoming – how could it? It's my own mess and I must accept the fact. On the other hand I cannot see this situation prolonging itself indefinitely. I am simply marking time now."

"My poor colleague," he said drily, but with all sincerity. There was no trace of irony in his tone – for he felt the same sharp pang which touched the heart of Blanford whenever he caught sight of her downcast head and averted eyes. But he at least was not abreast of the developments which she had outlined for the benefit of Jourdain. It is difficult to know what he would have thought of them – elation, sympathy, horror? The repertoire of the human heart is a vast one, a veritable broom-cupboard. She had left the car in the little square with its silent trees and small white church which enshrined so many memories of the past. Jourdain had extracted a firm promise that she would dine with him soon in his rooms.

She stood for a while letting the atmosphere of the little square seep into her, seep through her mind.

How long life seemed when one thought of the past – especially of all those sadly wasted years of war and its distresses. Her friend Nancy Quiminal used also to visit the little church. During the *fêtes votives* she brought posies of flowers to offer on behalf of an old aunt who had been born in the village of Montfavet, and had attended catechism classes in the church, which hadn't changed a jot. Constance tried the door.

She sat there in a pew for a long moment, counting her quiet heart beats, almost without drawing breath. The immense weariness of the war years had not yet quite dissipated, while the present with its problems seemed hopelessly lacklustre. Had they come back too soon to recapture some of the *élan* and optimism of the past – had they made a fatal miscalculation? It was true perhaps that one should never try to go back to retrace one's steps to a place where one has once been happy.

A wave of depression came over her, and for a moment she was almost tempted to say a prayer of abject self-commiseration, pagan though she was. She smiled at the impulse, but compromised by crossing herself as she stood before the watchers in the painting. Who knows? It was gipsy country and the piety might work like a *grigri* . . . Then she resumed her little borrowed car and set off back to collect Sutcliffe whom she had left in town to do some shopping with Blanford.

But when she found her way back to the little tavern by the river which was their point of rendezvous she was furious to find them both drunk – not "dead" drunk but in an advanced state of over-elaboration. Blanford could be most irritating when he became slightly incoherent while Sutcliffe became simply cryptic. They had been absorbing that deleterious brew known to the peasantry as *riquiqui*, a fire-water compounded of several toxins. "O God!" she said in dismay. "You are both drunk!" At which they protested energetically though with a slight incoherence which gave the show away. "*Au contraire*, my dear," said Blanford, "this is the way my world ends, not with a bang but a Werther. First time I've tasted this stuff. It's plebeian but very con-soling. *Vive, les enfants du godmichet*!" Sutcliffe at once said, "I echo that toast in all solemnity. Did you know that for several centuries the city kept its renown because twelve churches preserved the authentic foreskin of Jesus as a holy relic? Twelve different foreskins, but each one the true and authentic . . ." They had set aside the pack of cards with which they had proposed to kill the time waiting for her. "A smegma culture," said Blanford gravely, thoughtfully, and his friend said, "When I hear the word I reach for the safety catch of my hair-spray. Levels of nonentity rise with a rising population. Who is going to do our dying for us? I once knew a parson who found he could not stand the sight of a freshly opened grave; he had a serious nervous breakdown. His doctor said soothingly, 'For a congenital worrier there is nothing more worrying than having nothing to worry about.' The poor parson jumped into the river." Blanford fiddled with his purchases and said, "When I killed you in the novel I intended to leave some ambiguity about the matter. Your body and the horse were washed up in Arles. But the police were to find that the dental imprints on your washed-up body did not coincide with the records of your London dentist. A pretty mystery!"

But to do justice to Blanford it must be allowed that underneath the tugging of the alcohol with its spurious consolation there echoed on the profound sense of desolation and emptiness which followed upon the defection (if that is the word) of Constance, and her absorption in Sylvie. As for the programme for a future life *à trois* . . . it was problematical in the extreme. "It was anguish to revisit Tu Duc," he told Sutcliffe. "The great dewy orchard, its apples tight and sweet as nuns' bums. And ironically I arrived with the first cuckoo – it seemed as if the whole spring had come to Avignon to announce my cuckoldry!"

It was with difficulty that she managed to shepherd them back to the car. Sutcliffe swore that his armpits were smoking from the *riquiqui*. But they were docile enough to obey her.

TWO

The Moving Finger

URING THESE DAYS OF SOMEWHAT FORCED CON-
viviality Constance realised that Blanford was
inwardly quite terrified of the move and all that it
might portend. He had begun to drink rather heavily, and of
course his bondsman and double followed suit – which made
them excellent company for Toby and a trial to Lord Galen
whose sense of humour was somewhat limited.

Paradoxically enough, however, the alcohol had an
enlivening effect on his talent and the commonplace book
began to fill up once more with what Sutcliffe called "thimbles"
or stray thoughts, and Blanford "threads". He wrote: "Pearls
can exist without a thread but the novel is an artefact and needs
a thread upon which to thread not so much the pearls as the
reader! It is not true that all the great themes have been used
up. Each age produces new ones. For us considerations like
this: what did they think, the women who watched the
crucifixion? They say that Buddha's wife became his first
initiate as did the daughter of Pythagoras. Those were the
days! Or, to change topics: what of the one Spartan to outlive
Thermopylae? He was left for dead on the field and came to
himself when the enemy had gone. But he could not stand the
odium of having escaped the slaughter, the suspicion of
having run away. He killed himself in despair. A Don Juan
who was terrified of women? Crusoe through the eyes of
Friday? A Life of Jesus out of Freud and vice versa?" Sutcliffe broke in with: "And love? What about love?" In his
new mood of sorrow and guilty intransigence Blanford said,
"The greatest of human illusions. It's not worth the kisses it
is printed on! Pearls before swine, what!"

"I am meditating a love story about the ideal couple. She would be called Rosealba, a girl to detonate insight if ever there was one. He – I haven't chosen a name yet, but he is the original death-yield of a love-bundle bang-plus-whimper man. Moreover it is a perfect marriage. Every morning he tells her something she does not know. Every evening he puts something so big and warm into her hand that she becomes thoughtful. They are almost dead from pure yes-ness. She has filled his heart with a glorious blindness."

Blanford protested, "It is out of date. The new discrete image of fiction is different. All the people are parts of larger people or composed of parts of smaller people, enlarged or diminished according to need. All events are the same event from a different angle. The work becomes a palimpsest with a laying out of superposed profiles. (My God! What supreme, prize-winning boredom! Nevertheless *avec cela j'ai fait mon miel!*)"

"The fourth-century Thebans were renowned for the practice of male sexual cohabitation – plus a crucial military innovation. The Sacred Legion comprising 150 homosexual couples was commanded by Pelopidas. It was the *corps d'élite* of the line regiments, and the only full-time unit. Perhaps your escaped legionary from Thermopylae committed suicide for other reasons: like the loss of his love?"

"Perhaps. I am reminded of some lines by Shakespeare: 'The fulcrum of my lover's bum / Will guarantee a nightmare come.' "

"Pelopidas."

"The first thing I do when I get up in the morning is to count my uniforms and run through my decorations, always starting with the Grand Bandage of Outer Mongolia where I was consul for a week. The artist decorated is an awesome sight. Should the poet make reassuring noises? Yum yum, yes please!"

"The sea-shell is the mystic's telephone. Only in the

sea-shell can one hear the mystical *toc sonore* and realise fully that in art a methodical licence rules, and that greatness does not stint but neither is it profligate. Finally that with every breath, every pulse-beat, every thought the whole universe invests its strength anew in reality. My friend, these bold words were dictated to me while I slept."

"In a new age of plastic caryatids we shall be permitted to change women in mid-scream. Thus to honour a secret goddess in her kilt of dead rats! Ah, you had better tear this letter up before reading it. Constance, the vatic second state you so distrust is reached without strain. I drifted into my life like an air-bubble into an old aorta. Went off bang one day and died for her. Exploded like an aneurism."

"Thank God for petrol. Arabs who are sensitive people buy women like others buy paintings. If paintings could open their legs they would buy paintings!"

But this persiflage could not disguise the deep unhappiness of the inward monitor. "I feel that I am giving off a steady glow of sex – like an abandoned dungheap!" said the incorrigible Sutcliffe. "And I have discovered a way of making Galen cry when he irritates me too profusely. Any reference to his late cat 'the wombat' puts him into a tearful state. When I twist the knife and speak of the 'old days' he whips out his hanky and says, 'Don't go on: we were so happy. I feel so lost now. Boo hoo!' He is highly susceptible, our great Co-ordinator."

"Other problems. How to defend yourself against your own self-esteem, eh? How not to look complacent when you are? There must be a gadget. The objective of the Christian is to be good, that of the Buddhist to be free. A different frequency. As death closes in more and more, illustrates itself with the loss of friends, the difference becomes more marked, one tends to take out more fire insurance. The mysterious root-force which gives enduring life to art can be felt and described in terms of architectonics, but its nature and essence remain mysterious – a dark river flowing from nowhere to nowhere. The pen touching paper marks the point of intersection merely. But when the artists of an age begin to use architectonics without humility we are in danger of losing the thread they weave. Wagner, Picasso – they are like mechanised muezzins whose prayers are recorded and broadcast on an almost political level. The intimacy has gone, the sensual exchange is not there. A microphone has intervened. As for the artist . . . poor fellow, after birth the terror of ego-consciousness strikes, the awe invades, the fear, and immediately the self laps itself in layer after layer of protective feelings to avoid foundering: like an onion, layer upon layer of defensive schemes. This is what poor old Buddha tried to counter by his policy of unwrapping the poor ego from its mummy-like swaddling clothes – the nervous aggressive reactions. He had made a capital discovery, but it is hard to convince people that the threat of nature is illusory. Yet once they twig the fact peace spreads round them in rings. But it's a whole art, to make yourself thoroughly vulnerable, even open towards death. Yes, once you are in the know nothing much matters any more, the penny has dropped. You realise that harmlessness is the highest good."

"Good art is never explicit enough."

"How should it be? It does not contain an ethic. You cannot break the code of the beauty exemplified by the rose. Ah! blessed principle of Indeterminacy which renders every eventual second of time miraculous: because all creation is arbitrary, capricious, spontaneous. Without forethought or afterthought."

"Every two seconds a mental defective is born. Nevertheless I pat the whole universe on the back and cry, 'Well done, old cock, well done!' "

"A monkey telling its nits, the priest his beads. Yet

somewhere I am sure the Great Plan exists. It is pinned out on a vast wall-map containing every imaginable reference as to our entries, exits, names, styles, natures, destiny. I'm sure!"

"You remind me of poor Quatrefages!"

"Yes. And his great map of the Templars. He has retired into the fastnesses of Montfavet – *la vie en rose*! He has not quite succeeded in convincing Galen that there is no Templar treasure to be exploited, but very nearly. The real secret treasure was the Grail, the lotus of insight. They had become infected first by the old Gnosticism so rampant in the Middle Orient (*outremer*); and then secondly and definitively by the practices of yoga – as the thread woven from millet round their waists so clearly showed. The Catholics were quite right – they *were* heretics, and their practices *did* create a danger for the Catholic world."

"Galen must be beside himself with anguish, after having invested so much money in futile research on the subject. So indeed must be the Prince who allowed himself to be talked into the scheme. We shall see next week when he arrives."

"They will find something else – a new line in widows and orphans. The war has created so many."

"A world without man – how was it before we emerged, I often wonder? Perhaps trees were the original people, anterior to humankind. Man sprang from the humus when it was mixed with water. Thus the mystics desire to regress into the unassailability of plant life – the insouciant lotus – in order to recapture the down-drive into dissolution, echoing the force we call gravity upon body and mind. What would you say to that? Excellence – the very notion of excellence comes from rarity, scarcity, paucity. Nature's robust mutations encourage species to evolve and lead the many towards the unique one. Ah! The brain's old begging-bowl! Perhaps the first fish were soluble and could not resist the rubbing water: but gradually by will-power and curiosity they learned survival. And elephants like humble space-ships floated without touching the ground . . ."

"Then came man. Woman blows man like spun glass from her womb. He is the weaker of the two, she writes his books though he executes them. Yet his sperm is her supreme document. If the quality falls off she becomes sick with malnutrition, soul-hunger, a sort of vampirism possesses her. The couple, the basic brick of understanding, is at risk. What is compromised is the sexual bonding which comes with insight."

"St Augustine was right in a way, writing letters to his punch-bag and cheeking the Holy Ghost. He was right – those who say don't know, those who know can't say . . . The corollary is that those who don't bloody know can't bloody say, yet today they make the most noise."

At this point Lord Galen erupted, clapping his hands, and said: "That is enough higher thought for today, Aubrey. Lunch is on the table, and it's mushrooms we picked ourselves."

THREE

The Prince Arrives

GALEN PLEADED WITH SUCH HEARTRENDING EMOTION for them to defer their departure that Constance took pity on him and decided to stay until the Prince arrived on the scene, which he duly did, accompanied by the newest version of Felix Chatto, now a man of the world, indeed a young ambassador in bud waiting for his Latin American republic to mature, so to speak. But the Prince was in an evil mood due to this latest contretemps with the British who had arrested twenty-five members of the secret brotherhood on the vague presumption that their activities were political and, by the same token, subversive. But for his part he was delighted to see Constance again and embraced her tenderly with tears in his eyes. He had left the princess behind in Cairo – she risked nothing from the British, he explained, as she had always been neutral; besides, she had become a bosom friend of the present ambassador, and as usual the embassy was at loggerheads with the army, as personified by the odious security brigadier who had initiated all these persecutions. "Him and an odious little man, Telford, who was a billiard marker in peace time and now enjoys currying favour with the army by supplying false information. He doesn't even speak a word of Arabic or Greek. And he's from Barnsley. I ask you, *Barnsley*!" He positively sizzled with contempt. "The real problem is, *how* can I go on loving my dear British when they let wretched people like this persecute us, eh?" He kissed her hands repeatedly, and she knew he was thinking of Affad, though he did not mention him. Instead he said: "And the boy?"

The boy had settled down very comfortably, having

found companions of his own age at the farm. He had been instantly adopted by the farmer and his wife, and made free of the place. What more intoxicating place than a farm with all its livestock to fire the mind of a child? But he had also, in some curious way, adopted Blanford; he had begun to show a preference for his company over the others'. Often when Aubrey was lying down – an enforced rest or siesta, say, for his back – the boy would appear and ask to be read to. Or he wished to play a game, or learn how to play backgammon. Blanford found this profoundly touching, and at once complied. It was as if Constance herself had asked him for these trifling favours. He loved the boy with this transferred love, the rival of Sylvie, so to speak. He wondered what it would be like to have a child of his own – he supposed that there was no experience in life so strange and so unique as to create another human being. Once the boy said, "You will stay with us, won't you?" and he was surprised for he supposed that the child had overheard some of their deliberations, their expressed doubts and hesitations. "Would you like that?" he said, feeling absurdly moved and flattered. The boy nodded in solemn fashion. "You play games so nicely," he explained, "and you always explain things to me!" An obscure shyness prevented him from recounting any of this to Constance. But she noticed for herself – small touches of affection and confidence marked the relation; when out walking in the courtyard, for example, the boy might take the hand of Blanford in an absentminded way; or break step in order to let their footsteps chime. On the other hand the embraces of Sylvie, which were on the effusive side, made the child ever so slightly impatient – anxious to be released. It was a strange polarity of inner feelings, yet it must have been based on some sort of sense of discrimination and insight, for when Felix Chatto arrived he was immediately accepted on the same basis by the boy, and instantly. About Felix Blanford was not surprised – he had developed into a most charming human being. A little bit of professional success and a sortie into the social world where he might receive the favours of women and so assume himself and gain confidence – it had served him in good stead, and he had not wasted his time. His scope had broadened with his new charm; even his looks had changed, had improved. He was lean and brown now in physique and with a high sense of irony, as befitted somebody in diplomacy, where one is always in danger of being besotted by protocol and caution. And a wry sense of humour set off to perfection his shy and self-deprecating manner. Most important of all he had managed now to get upon even terms with Lord Galen and was no more oppressed and intimidated by the shadow of the great man. He was able to stand his ground and have opinions of his own. The boot was, in fact, on the other foot, for Lord Galen had become diffident and hesitant with *him*, and of late had started to defer to *his* opinions. Indeed he had even been invoked to bring some critical judgement to bear upon the Templar Treasure investment – was it worth continuing the quest, or should it be given up as useless? The debate which was now going to ensue upon the matter would largely turn upon his private opinion as to the soundness of the venture. Time had enabled him to turn the tables on his seniors. All this put him into a very good humour, enabled him to support with sangfroid the Prince's own dark humour. But it was evident that on the question of their so-called investment he harboured more doubts than hopes, despite the tantalising elements which Quatrefages had revealed in the construction of his Templar wall-map, despite the reluctance of Lord Galen to relinquish all hope of finding a treasure buried in the crypt of some old castle. "I shall be sorry to play the 'killjoy'," he told Blanford, "but good sense is good sense, particularly in finance!"

"Finance again!" cried Sutcliffe later that night. "But

did Felix tell you of his mission to China, to help advise them on how to balance their budget? Galen sent him from Geneva. Did he?" Blanford shook his head. Overwhelmed by his excitement, Sutcliffe tapped his own temples with a clenched fist, but softly, and said: "I will, then. My goodness, what an adventure for Felix.

"When he arrived he found them all convulsed with enthusiasm for Zen Buddhism, of all things! Yes, I know, I know. In the Marxist Ministry of Finance they had never heard of such a thing. But they were working with an American adviser called O'Schwartz if you please and he had told them that the only future for China lay in tourism. They must provide facilities and he, O'Schwartz (he said he was from an old Irish family, Madison Avenue Irish) would guarantee the tourists. All America would rush to visit China, but it must have not only accommodation but also sports like tennis, golf, water skiing, etc., and Zen Buddhism. They looked puzzled and asked what the devil that might be. They'd never heard of it. Well, O'Schwartz told them that everyone knew what it was, it was kinda religious only needed no effort. He knew that there was money in it because the Rothschilds were on to it and it was given away free with every packet of crisps by the Club Mediterranée. Now the American tourist insisted on the best and nothing but; if he did not find Zen on the menu he would feel he was being cheated. Obediently they got to work and a professor was found who had heard of the article. He told them of the epoch-making arrival of Bodhidharma from India, where he had been the twenty-eighth patriarch, in order to become the first in China. Dazed, they heard him describe the long incubation in the cave, where the sage sat facing a blank wall for so many years until the King asked him what he had gained from the practice, only to be told, 'Nothing at all, your Majesty!' This really baffled the Chinese, but O'Schwartz stuck to his guns, and they turned to Felix for confirmation of the fact that American tourists would feel happier if they could visit, for example, the original cave or the original wall. They had sent out scouts to try and locate the original cave where the practice of Zazen was first initiated. In the meantime, while waiting for news of it, they addressed themselves to the formidable problems raised by the other requisites – the large hotels, beaches, excursions, shopping centres. Finally word came back that a cave – perhaps the original, perhaps not – had been found and was open for their inspection. But it was a long way off and would necessitate a long journey by train and jeep and finally mule. The old sage never did things by halves. It was remote, this cave. Felix was full of misgivings, but O'Schwartz was adamant. They must really take the trouble to look at it on behalf of future tourist activities. In fairness to the Ministry it must be said that they did not insist on the *original* cave – it was the relentless American adviser who did. Any bit of wall, any cave, would do, thought the Ministry. But at the prompting of O'Schwartz the Professor took charge of them and off they set on a long journey by river and pure jungle towards the keystone of the old sage's edifice. Wild country, yes, and full of rock-panthers of a beautiful ivory hue which they caught sight of from time to time, but rarely for they were shy and of a guilty conscience. This animal delights in the flesh of dogs, just as man does in the flesh of fowls. At first they divined their invisible presence as they advanced because their dogs began to disappear one by one, and noiselessly, with hardly a bark or a shriek; they melted into invisibility as if some unknown hand had sifted them away. It was unnerving – like swimmers taken by a shark. Once or twice they caught a glimpse of these favoured great creatures which seemed to have stepped out of an old engraving or a wash drawing of the middle period. At night they drew close about the fire which they were forced to light in the wilderness in order to keep the panthers at bay. They slept badly with their huddle of dogs. It was wild country with no towns and no taverns. So at last they came to the place of the cave.

The old scholar who led the party was a vague and prosy old gentleman whose exposition was blurred and whose knowledge was full of gaps. Fortunately Felix knew a little and O'Schwartz also. As for Bodhidharma the only painting extant is too late to have been done from life. The sage's eyes are crossed from his exertions. Diplopia giving the impression of the pineal eye, the Third Eye in full flower. The only painting shows the tender clown with painted tears engrossed on his face, fixed like the flared nostrils of painted rocking-horses uprearing to the winds of heaven. When the poor little king, so thirsty for instruction, asked old Bod just what forty years of speechless wall-gazing had done for him, the great one returned a somewhat dusty answer. 'Forget it, cod,' he said, or words to that effect. There was in fact nothing that *could* be predicated about the experience he had been through. Either one twigged or not; there was nothing to say about so private an inkling of truth. The King sighed. (Was memory then so tenacious? The keystone to the average human condition was, as always, stress and fret and frenzy. The squalid and chubby self was still in the centre of the picture.)

Zazen, as he christened it, was the dire and absolute procedure which enabled him to effect a breakthrough into the other register of consciousness – the open realm or field where the whole of consciousness floated, detached and sub-lime. The cave they had found was large and silent, its walls like superb natural frescos of blood-red stone – intricate interlacings almost suggesting a human hand's work. It was not here that he squatted, the sage, for these graffiti could have reminded him of things, and he was not allowed to have either associations or even memories. His purified outlook upon the sublime was empty of every qualification! He was glimpsing the very 'itness' of things, of all nature, if you wish. He plucked this dense wall as one plucks a goose, or a picker picketh fruit or moss, absently present all the time. This kind of reality had no Therefore in it. Bodyless, Boneless, Soundless and Meaningless – it was full of information for his parched intuition. Reality now was sweet as a plum, romantic as wedding cake among these neolithic veins of gorgeous stone which he rejected in favour of a barren uncoloured strip of cave. A far corner which was not declamatory, which was worth its weight in ... The tremendous plumage of nonentity – gazing into it he realised all the riches of his inmost dowry. All Sesame slid back – it was a simply mental knack to slide the panel back upon the mirror of truth! The place, so ordinary for him, would become hallowed through the bald irreverence of the horde. Early tourists must have come. They visited bones until they dissolved into dust. Then with moistened finger they licked up his dust or supposed dust. Now only the wall remained on view for a century or two – orders of the Ministry. But 'Is this *really* all there is to see?' they ask the guide. Perhaps one could X-ray the wall, and catch a glimpse of the treasures inside? No, since then man has lived on in ever-increasing embarrassment at this power-cut in the central vision. The travel agencies can do nothing except repeat promises of their good faith. It is not the original wall – it proved to be too far away; so they settled for a cave which was more easily accessible to the tourist. But the original – Felix was aware of the importance of the experience O'Schwartz had given him, and he was duly grateful. In the silence of the cave he stood and counted the golden register of his lagging heartbeats. He could not help but think in quotation either – Plato's mystical cave with its shadows loomed up in memory. Plato's cave was the un-purged cave of human consciousness. The soul's bargain

basement which old B. had turned into a jumble sale! Fecit!
With only his eyeballs for probes he exhausted the contents
of the blank wall by a relentless attention to its focal beauty.
Plucking a blank wall with primal sight – a wall dense with
music like some carnal plum. This is what gave the old lad
his fatal ZA – his *do-re-me-fa-so*! What he was rewarded
with was something that would not melt in silence, nor
pucker in wind, nor be honed by mischief-makers, nor
claimed by clowns. Within it all polarities ceded. Never was
it to be disavowed by the wrong love.

In this critical wall he saw a mirror reflecting the whole
retrievable inward chaos of man. He harnessed the energy it
gave off, fully aware that one day local fame would become
world renown; yet the plight of human happiness could not
be changed by simply changing the metaphors for desire. The
real original sin of the affect was trying to perpetuate the
transitory. Water, itself the symbol of ancient purity, stag-
nates without motion, without movement. This was old B.'s
simple ZA! Hunting down an old spontaneousness which had
once been innate, unrehearsed: pining to dwell once more,
and this time for ever, in a perfected nonchalance of being!
This he managed to do with the bare bodkin of his human
probe – his eyeballs. The old TU QUOQUE gave place to rest
and silence. As he told the king: 'Imitate plants in their
defencelessness. If you are a love-child it doesn't matter if
your father is only a groom. The art of fishing is never to let
the fish know that you are in love with it! To heighten
pleasure tighten pain. The highest sensuality lies in repressing
the hunger.' What marvels of insight emerge from privation!
What a marvellous topic was silence! (The king burst into
tears. He had tried so *hard* and here he was: out of his depth!)
All these aphorisms, the spawn of insight! It was such bad
taste – altogether too literary. The soft reversal of the real
provokes a wholesome vertigo in the opinionated. The hairpin

bends where death attends. The secret plumage of the rock gave him the information that he needed. He marvelled at the sapience of his triumphant ZA! There was no written text, no code for this passion. A slip of the pen in the dog-days of love – he now knew how to be vigilant in silence and quite sorrowless. The sources of culture were obvious now. The origin of all drama was incest! The role of the physician was to purge our childhood of wishes.

There he sat, the old crystal-chafer, quietly rubbing his soft lampoon and daring humanity to dare."

The dry copyist's succinct word for human craving – four letters beginning with an L. Lust? Lost? Last? List? Live? Love? The choice is extensive yet intensive. The whole of this experience, the strange journey, the cave, the zany propositions of the Marxists, exercised a strange effect upon Felix; he felt changed in some profound way, but he could not have said just how. And for once he felt unwilling to discuss the experience, except to make fun of its bizarre side – the thought of Americans with cameras plodding through this field. O'Schwartz had even evolved a scheme by which they could obtain certificates of religious initiation in the Dharma – he had suborned a Californian monk to help him with his scheme. Thus the tourist would have something to show when he got home – apart from his photographs. A diploma!

Something to show! A certificate of higher indolence! Felix recounted this whole spiritual adventure to Galen who listened with an air of pained puzzlement. It was evident that the chances for speculative investment were poor and somewhat chancy with those Chinks – moreover brainwashed Chinks of the left hand! Yet . . . they were right about tourism, he should suppose, if only communications opened up once more and the war-damage was set to rights. "What does the Prince think?" he asked a little plaintively, and Felix replied, "He is in a bad mood and says that he won't chance a penny on any Chinese scheme. On the other hand he is reluctant to relinquish the Templar treasure scheme. He still thinks there is hope of a breakthrough towards a real treasure. Myself, I . . ." His shrugged shoulders were quite eloquent enough. But meanwhile the Prince had come into the room silently and was in time to overhear the exchange. "It is not quite my point of view," he said rather testily, "but you must remember that I come from a land where the bazaars are absolutely crammed with lying soothsayers. I consulted one in the Grand Bazaar in Cairo in the middle of the night by the weird light of those large hissing acetylene lamps which make everyone look deathly pale, drained of blood! And what Aubrey calls 'squirms' of children jumping about like fleas. Now this old man was extremely explicit about this whole venture. He told me I was involved in a treasure-hunting scheme about which I had become somewhat doubtful, wondering whether to abandon hope. He said that I must not give up for at least another six months. He could not tell me whether the treasure really still existed, because he was too far away from the scene, but he suggested that I consult someone who was actually on the spot. That is why I hurried up and planned my arrival for May."

"Why May specially?" asked Galen and received the laconic reply: "The gipsy festival rounds off May, remember?" Galen did not but he pretended he did. Felix nodded and provided the exact date and the exact place: Les Saintes Maries de la Mer! "I will have our fortunes retold by a gipsy," said the Prince, "and we'll see whether to carry on or abandon the whole investment!"

"Fortune-telling?" said Galen somewhat unhappily. "It's not very *sound*, is it? I mean to say, having your palm read, what?" The Prince nodded his agreement to the proposition. "Nevertheless," he said with resolution, "there is so much that is questionable about the whole enterprise that one little soothsayer won't change much. I don't intend to abandon the *Financial Times*. But the one in Cairo told me I had a partner who was too cautious, believed too much in moderation. Said I must encourage him to risk more. How do you like that?"

Galen put on his wounded look. "Well, I like that!" he said reproachfully, "after all we have put up. As for lying soothsayers, we have had our share with the myth-making of young Quatrefages. And we still don't know where we are!"

But about the gipsies the Prince was not wrong, for already their slow steady infiltration into the province had begun – a leisurely penetration into Avignon and thence into the Camargue. It was probably deliberate, in order not to alarm the country people too much by a violent gipsy presence – though in smaller villages the church bells might be rung and the housewife's cry go up: "The gipsies are coming!" It was the signal to bolt and bar the granary or the barn, to get your washing off the line, and to withdraw from the window sills such items of common fare as pots of basil or of wild mint, so renowned were they for their light-fingered tactics and the brilliant insolence of their approach to the timid and the law-abiding. They invested the little towns of the Midi as cunningly as freebooters might – for that is what they were. The women would sell baskets or profess to grind your knives for you at your front door: but your eye must be sharp for while one swarthy beauty worked at the knife blades another might slip past you into the house and pilfer. But they were so good-looking and insolent and dressed like birds of paradise that one was always torn between fear and admiration, while the beauty of the women set the sap mounting in the veins of the menfolk. They were not averse to some quick sexual commerce in a barn or in the woods – fair reason for your wife's anxiety when the cry went up that they had arrived. *They did not seem to care!* That is what went home like a knife-thrust in the heart of the careworn house-wife! In their dusky skins and glowing eyes they seemed to express the perils as well as the joys of absolute freedom. Yet for all their being scattered far and wide there was only one festival a year at which they were all joined together to honour their patron saint, the dark-skinned Sara whose grottoes were in the crypt of the little Church of the Saintes Maries de la Mer, the famous village on the sea to which all their steps were now bending. But first they filled up Avignon and for a while created a kind of excited tremor in the life of the merchants and settled folk. A gipsy fiddler in the main square managed to inflame some young couples to dance to his music – he was of a northern strain and sounded Hungarian, or rather his music did. They were getting them-selves assembled in their various troupes to await the arrival of their Queen Mother who was somewhere on the road still.

Without her there could be no fête for the moon-people – for the gipsies are lunar folk. So they marked time, reading hands and tea leaves and coffee grounds until she should come.

Gradually, too, the town woke up to their exciting and distressing presence and the inevitable reaction, set in in the form of increased police surveillance and minor harassments and persecutions at camping sites and in urban squares or wherever a cart and a tent appeared. In olden times – yet not so long ago – they would have been arrested, imprisoned or whipped at a cross-roads for flouting the common law, for trespassing and pilfering. Today they only had to endure a minor form of the old rabid persecution – the object being to expel them, force them to move on. There was no need for harsher measures since everyone knew that their objective was not Avignon but Les Saintes, and that they would soon ebb quietly away towards the torrid plains of the Camargue. The town was simply a staging post for the grand march southward. But it offered an extraordinary glimpse into the organisation of this mysterious ethnic group. "In one of your previous lives I learned about them from a girl called Sabine," said Sutcliffe as they sat before their glasses of wine on the broad terrace above the olive grove. Blanford nodded: "I well remember," he said, "and I have often wondered what happened to her. They said that she had gone off with a gipsy." Blanford chuckled. "It was the fashionably romantic thing to say or even to do then: before the war, I mean." Yet it had been more than that, for Sabine had been told that she was descended from the famous gipsy personage Faa, who was among the first to establish a right of entry into America. Sutcliffe refilled his glass and went on in reminiscent vein: "In my wine-jumbled brain I remember not only her favours, surprisingly tender and vulnerable, but also her conversation. I had vaguely thought of them as persecuted people simply because they would not keep still, would not integrate with settled communities. But the long saga of persecution – I had not realised to the full what that had meant to them. It had formed them and rounded them until their personalities were as solidly obdurate as an ingot. They have become incapable of change."

The Prince was listening with great attention to this somewhat drunken disquisition. "Nevertheless," he said, "in Egypt they are a sly and slippery folk – and their name is apparently derived from *gypt*, which is 'us'. If they are, as you say, unchangeable it is because they *are* change. They are like water and will take any shape, but always stay the same. And by the way, I was talking to a minor functionary of the *mairie* today and he was saying how amazing it was that so many tribes manage to get down to the Saintes for this Saint Sara festival every year. They even come from behind the Iron Curtain as you must have seen from some of the carts. Strange folk!"

But doubtless they themselves would look almost as strange *en masse* for they had hired a large red motor bus for the excursion, complete with driver. It was the Prince's idea, as he had been told of the almost intolerable congestion of traffic caused by the slow-moving carts and the horses – not to mention the vast plumes of dust which rose along the gipsies' passage, following them like a forest fire. A van such as this would free them from the responsibilities of the road and also keep them all together in a single party. Needless to say, the preparations for the trip involving hampers of elaborate food and wine put everyone into a good humour while the Prince devised ever more wonderful configurations of truffled trifles with which to tease the palates of the pilgrims – for they conceived themselves now as such. After all, they had a purpose, they were voyaging with the intention of invoking Saint Sara, asking her to take a sounding for them in the ocean of futurity. Travelling like this, in a congregation, so to speak, enabled the more loquacious (or simply drunker?) members among them to permit themselves sonorous disquisitions upon whatever subject came to hand. But the thought of the vanished Sabine touched off other reminiscences of gipsy lore and history with which the nostalgic Sutcliffe enlivened the first part of the journey through the flowering meads of high Provence which soon gave place to the sadder, flatter plains of the Camargue – country of marsh and rivulet and lake where flies and mosquitoes abounded, as well as the sturdy brown bulls of the locality which were raised as cockade fighters for the Provençal bull rings. Here too the characteristic cowboy of the land, the *gardien*, prevailed with his broad-brimmed sombrero and the trident which he sported like a sceptre of office. As the straggling columns wound dustily through his land to the sea there was need for constant watchfulness, for the gipsies were light-fingered and pilfered remorselessly while the strangers' dogs teased the bulls and snapped at the horses – the little white palaeolithic steeds which the poets of the place always saw in terms of a foam flowing over the land like waves on the blue sea which lay ahead, the crown of their journey, the church of Saint Sara.

"I feel wonderful on this wine," said the relentless double of Blanford. "I may have a tendency to boom a bit. If I do, curb me with a frown, will you?"

"I will. Anyway I see no mystery in the Gyps because I think of them as Jews gone wild. No money sense."

"Oh dear!" said Lord Galen unhappily. "Now you will start being anti-Jewish. I feel it coming. Change the subject, please!" Sutcliffe poured him out a glass which he drank off.

So they voyaged on in a pleasant state of abstraction, skimming as much as they could along the swarthy columns of "Greek" and "Egyptian" and "Romanian" and "Bulgarian" gipsies, each tribe with its characteristic music and avocation – basketwork for the "French", pots and pans for the "Greek" farriers.

Some of the horse-drawn caravans were brilliantly painted, speaking of Sicily or England. And by the wayside perched their tents in small encampments where the children lay about like litters of cats and puppies in the bluish dust. The tide, however, flowed steadily towards the sea where the little church of the Saint stuck out its abrupt butt towards the beaches, never quite allowing one to forget that it was originally a fort, a defence against the pirates who ravaged this coast. As for the beaches themselves they had become one great single encampment, as if they had been spawned by the grand Souk of Cairo. Here the various races mingled and bickered, the various musics contended against each other – and also with the noise of the waves forever bursting upon the white sand. "From Messina to the Baltic, from Russia to Spain, this people had been enslaved, tortured, often put to

death: their lives were worth nothing. Long past the sixteenth
century the persecutions endured. Indeed at that time anyone
who frequented or succoured them was listed as a common
felon and could be put to death without even the benefit of a
jury." Blanford dredged up this scrap from some old conversation, from perhaps Sabine? Her name had come back to
hover about him like a persistent fly: he wondered what had
happened to her. And, of course, as is always the case, he was
soon to meet her in the flesh again and find out!

So the little bus struggled on through the dust plumes
until the broad beaches came in sight, framed by the rocking
sealine. Their horses and carts had taken possession of the
beaches under the watchful eye of the local cavaliers who by
now had become familiars, wandering among the tents on
their little white steeds. A great fair was growing up around
the event which would end with a religious service and the
transport of the three Maries down to the sea on a great
wooden trestle banked with flowers; the whole party, bursting
with ardour and joyful tears, plunging through the shallows
until the sea was breast-high, and the whole cavalcade seemed
to float on the water, encircled now by all the fisher boats of
the little seaport, appropriately bedecked and beflagged in
their honour.

Their own objective was one of the seaside cafés where
they had reserved a shady corner of terrace with a vast green
awning, which would serve as a headquarters from which
they could sally forth into the fair at will. Here their hampers
were unpacked, their plates and cutlery being disposed upon
long trestle tables – all the allure of a scouts' picnic. And it
was while they were taking their aperitifs that a gipsy woman
approached them with a slow and curious air, as if she were
looking for someone who might be found in their midst. She
was awakening into an uncertain familiarity with the face of
Blanford – though it was Sutcliffe who was the first to

recognise her, and let out a cry of recognition. "Sabine, darling!" he cried. "There you are at last! We've been hunting for you in each other's books for ages! Where have you been?" The woman thus addressed was indeed hardly recognisable when compared to the memories they had kept of the old Sabine.

She was stout and dirty and wrinkled, and her clothes and trinkets were of the cheapest sort. Her hair was greying now, and the once magnificent eyes were a prey to myopia, which added to her difficulty in recognising those who had once been acquaintances and friends. As they peered it seemed as if they were seeing her afresh through several veils of reality, several washes of colour. Of course she had always been rather self-consciously a tramp, as so many university children of her era had been. You showed your intellectual independence by not washing in that far-off epoch. But Sabine had gone further and actually disappeared with the gipsies, which had more or less destroyed the happiness and peace of mind of her father Lord Banquo. He for his part had been an old associate of Lord Galen and had even known the Prince. So that when Sabine discovered herself to them several recognitions took place and several simultaneous conversations broke out around her past and around her father, whose chateau in Provence was now boarded up and deserted and seemed to have stayed like that throughout the war. "He's dead, yes," she said in her harsh but calm tones – it was so strange to hear that Cambridge accent coming out of her swarthy face. "They say of course I killed him by taking to the road – well, perhaps I did. But there was no other choice for me to make. I wished to please him, and there was nothing I could offer as an excuse for my choice. I even submitted to a Freudian analysis of several months in order to get myself fully explained: but it explained nothing and I was literally driven to this solution in spite of myself. It wasn't love either, or passion, as in the novels. It was like one decides to go to America or into a monastery. It was a sort of magnetic solution. I was sleep-walking, and I still am. I would not change this for worlds." And surprisingly she put her hands on her fat hips and let off a laugh like a police siren. How much she had changed, thought Blanford, and he had a sudden memory of Banquo's face watching her with such admiration, such pain, such anxiety.

She sat down and put her head on one side, as if she were listening to herself; indeed she was. "God!" she said. "I'm so thirsty to speak some English after so long; and yet it sounds so strange coming out of my head. I thought I had forgotten it after so many years of dog-Esperanto. Aubrey, speak to me!" and she smiled this new hideous smile full of flashing gold teeth. She tugged his sleeve affectionately, pleadingly almost. He said, "Immediately I want to know *why*! Why did you do it?"

She lit a hemp cigarillo and began to smoke in short sharp inspirations, holding it not between her fingers but in the palm of her hand, as if it were a pipe. "I've told you," she said, "just as I told dear old Freud who was hunting my Oedipus complex. Mario, the man I went to was so much older, you see, that they thought he was a father-replacement. I ask you!" She laughed again in her new ferociously lustful way, and clapped her hand on his thigh. "When I came down from Cambridge I was an economics star and I wanted to do a study of society which would pinpoint whatever it was that was preventing us from constructing the perfect utopian state – a state so just and equitable that we were all using the same toothbrush. You know how it is when one is young? Idealism. I finally narrowed it all down to the idea of the Untouchable in his various forms. My book was going to analyse Untouchability. We were after all Jews, so it was a good starting point; then I went to India and experienced all the horrors of

Brahminism; finally among other little ethnic puzzles I came upon the gipsy, first in the caves at Altamira and then one day in Avignon when I bought a basket from a rough-looking gipsy in the main square of Avignon. The next day when I was passing through the same square he was still there and he recognised me. He said, 'Come with me, it is important. Our mother wants to speak to you. She says she *recognises* you.' This is our tribal mother – *puri dai*, as they call her! Our tribe is a matriarchy. This old woman took my hands and predicted that by the end of the summer I would join them and that Mario would make me pregnant – which he did. She forgot to add that he would also give me syphilis! But compared to so many other trials it was nothing and I was after all sufficiently educated to get it treated. I was spellbound by the self-evident fact that I *was* a gipsy – the whole of European culture slid from my shoulders like a cloak. Mario was much older but like an oak tree. After the first night in his tent I went home and told my father I was going to leave him." Yes, but her voice held pain at this stage in the story. Blanford remembered that troubled summer when the old man locked himself up and refused all invitations. How tough women were, finally!

Indeed she looked quite indestructible in the quiet certainty of her direction. "We've done India several times. All the horrors. And Spain and Central Europe. My children died of cholera. We burned them and moved on. We speak about economic survival and I am a trained economist. But where does it come from, the ethnic puzzle? Even Freud did not know, I found. But the gipsy has resources, he has to; because often one is moving through a land which, if not hostile, does not need our pots and pans, our woven rugs or rush baskets, or our farrier work or the knife grinding. What do you do then to eat? Mario taught me the economic answer." Here she was so overcome with laughter that the tears filled

74

her eyes. "It has been our mainstay in so many places. It is called the 'dog and duck act' in the annals of the American circus, and we even have a faded poster which we hang on the tent where it takes place." "I must see this," said Sutcliffe, and she said, "So you shall this evening. Our stars, our principals, are called Hamlet and Leda, and I sometimes think when I watch them coupling that they represent European culture – the ill-assorted couple, the basic brick of any culture; what sort of child could they make? Why, something like us!" The Prince was filled with an ardour and a compassion which showed that he recognised how remarkable a woman she was. "It is deeply affecting what you say!" he cried, brushing away a tear; and taking her hands he covered them with kisses. "It reminds me so much of Egypt!" he said. "I feel quite all-overish!" And he shuddered with intellectual admiration for this weird gipsy who was now quite at her ease – quietened by the hemp and full of joy to rediscover old friends who might well have been dead after such a long war . . . And she submitted to the Prince's admiration with great dignity of bearing, showing that she was touched and pleased to be understood. Yet how strange the English language sounded to her as it flowed out of her head.

"Hamlet is a small and apparently ageless and immortal fox-terrier, and Leda is a fat old goose, lazy and thoroughly lascivious as all geese are. But she loves being mounted by the dog, she ruffles her feathers with appreciation and honks while he, like a dog or a banker, gives of his best. I realised after the death of my own that they were really our children, our own small contribution to the way things are. How extraordinary the world is. Even God is dying of boredom – it's called entropy!"

"Don't say that!" exclaimed Lord Galen – a surprising interjection, coming from him – "Don't say that, please. There will be nothing left to invest in!" And now the church bells in the belfry of the fortress-church burst out in an anguish of clamour, almost as if they were answering Lord Galen's prayer! And Sabine laughed once more and said, "You must go and pay your respects to Sara now because soon the procession will begin and with such crowds you won't be able to move. Then come back here and I will try and arrange for you to be skried, or read or divined – however you like to put it – by someone reliable, perhaps even our Mother, because so many of us are cheats and rogues and bluffers. India too is thick with imposters and thieving swamis, as you well know!"

Sutcliffe murmured under his breath the folk verses they could never remember correctly.

> A slimy swami pinched his cap
> But Mrs Gilchrist gave him clap.

"No, no," said Blanford, "I swear my version is the correct one. I wish we could prove it!" And he recited the lines in another text.

> He swore the fairies gave him clap
> Though Mrs Gilchrist took the rap.

He added: "In this way the British Army made its small contribution to Indian thought. I wanted to write the biography of Mrs Gilchrist who set up the first classy tearoom-bordel in Benares and imported suburban butterflies from Peckham to staff it. But there was never enough material available."

As he was speaking they were all turning their heads towards the main street where there was a sudden eruption of music and a gush, literally a gush, of white steeds with flowing manes and the Camargue *gardiens* mounted on them, sombrero on head and trident in hand. They were to form the escort for the Saints in their descent to the sea, and they were clad rather

76

formally in the dress uniform of their profession – beautiful whipcord trousers with black piping, and flower-patterned shirts topped with black velvet coats, and short jackboots. It was a uniform which melted down two different influences into a harmonious and aristocratic unity – Spain and the Far West of America. At their appearance the guitars, rather hesitant at first, burst into a fury of passion and the air throbbed with the warmth of castanets and the swing of Andalusian dances, the whirl of skirts, the snapping of coloured paper streamers. There was just time to salute Sara, though after they had done so they wondered at their own courage in facing this dense press of swarthy bodies and literally carving a passage through it.

Sutcliffe was happy to renounce the adventure when he caught a glimpse of the throng hemmed in by the aisles of the little church, whose walls were decorated with every kind of *ex voto* imaginable, depicting shipwreck, accident, fires, earthquakes, acts of violence as well as acts of God; broken heads and limbs, dying children and their parents, overturned boats and horses destroyed by accident . . . a whole hospital of woes which had been either cured or averted by the Saint who was now waiting for them below stairs, clad in her new vestal gown. But how could they get to her? She stood on a trestle table at the far end of a low crypt or cellar where the lack of oxygen made one instantly begin to suffocate, while the brilliant wave of light from hundreds of candles throbbed and pulsed – for they too were eating your oxygen. Yet light one you must, and place it in the iron chandelier as well as deposit a coin in the offertory box hard by the statue. The dull plonking of coins in the wooden box provided an accompaniment to the low haunting chanting and moaning of the crowd, forever retreating and advancing towards the gorgeous black statue of the Saint. She is black, yes, but the cast of her features is completely European, occidental. Beauty and youth

and incorruptibility seem united in her lucent and happy gaze.
She looks through everything into a beyond of such perfect
felicity that one longs to make the journey with her. The
gipsies whimpered and sweated and crossed themselves and
muttered in an ecstasy of apprehension and requited love.
The other two saints were rather a washout – they were just
Biblical walk-on parts, but Saint Sara was bursting with
superb unction at what she knew. She looked a darling who
was simply burning to whisper the secret to someone – if only
there were less noise and singing and general rumpus – for a
thousand children added to the complications with their
chirping and shoving. And the whole of this sweating
humanity was pushed down into a little dark sinus of a crypt
where breathing was a torment. How did she not melt, one
wondered, for Sara was fashioned in black wax.

"Not for me," said Sutcliffe. "I can't face this sort of
thing. One hand on your pocket book and the other on your
balls . . . it's too much." So he elected to go for a walk among
the tents while the saints were being carried down to sea on
their wooden trestle – part of the traditional service.

The beaches were swarming with families who had
settled in for the usual three-day festival, around flourishing
camp fires where food was roasting on the spit. Sabine walked
with him, pausing from time to time to greet an acquaintance
or relation, and say a word to the children at their heels.

"Coming down through the chestnut forests of High
Provence we had a wonderful stroke of luck," she said, "for
we ran into an absolute colony of hedgehogs: you know that
for the gipsy it's the greatest delicacy of all. That's what you
are smelling now. Mario is doing three or four for lunch. We
dug out an old abandoned clay pit for the event. We gut them
and then cover them thickly in wet clay before putting them
to roast in a fire built just below ground. Have you ever eaten
them?" He had not. "Slightly richer than Chinese puppy but

very good in flavour. When the clay is baked and cooling it is knocked off with a hammer or a stone and all the quills and the skin go away with it, leaving the flesh exposed. I know – it must sound horrid!" For he shuddered at the description. "So I won't invite you for lunch today!"

"Sabine!" he said, suddenly stopping to look at her rather pathetically. "Darling, why did you leave me? You knew you loved me." She smiled and put a hand on his arm. "Of course I did," she said, "but you must ask Aubrey that; I could not take you with me, after all. Our lives were split down the middle, no way of joining them that I could see."

They stood for a long time thus, staring at each other while the crowds swirled round them, streaming down to the seashore in the wake of the Saints. Then they turned back against the human tide and in a quieter side street found a dark wine cellar full of barrels of local wine; and here at a dirty table they sat down and ordered a glass to drink. She was still talking with a kind of considered impetuousness, simply for the pleasure of talking English again. She seemed so real it was hard to think of her as purely imaginary. "And the big question is always 'Why?'" she said. "Starting with my surprised and half-incredulous father – old Banquo, as they called him in the City. I adopted it also as a form of address and it amused him. But this thing outraged him so, his sense of logic and reason. He knew a lot about gipsies and the relentless persecutions they had had to endure over the centuries. And there was one particularly savage tale which he thought might clinch the matter and dissuade me from the choice I had made. He had heard it first from an attaché of the Austrian Embassy in Sofia – you know he began as a diplomat, my father, and left the service because of the inadequate pay. In his first posting he met this little crippled Austrian – I even remember his name, Egon Von Lupian! They became friends despite the difference in age because both were mad about

orchids and collected them. Von Lupian was a leg short and
wore a wooden one with a spike in it which made – I quote –
a 'characteristic clicking sound' on the marble floors of the
old Chancery. He was a strange number – Aubrey has written
about him elsewhere. But he told my father about his childhood in Austria. He came of an ancient and aristocratic
family, and one of his uncles owned vast estates in the north.
He was a great hunter and often had the boy to stay with him.
He ran a great pack of stag-hounds in the barren marches of
his part of the country; and sometimes they would course
some poor wretch of a tramp who had strayed into their
lands. But the choice quarry was a gipsy, and if possible a
woman with a child at breast! Imagine. He remembers once
his uncle, a big red-faced man with a curling moustache
coming down to breakfast rubbing his hands and saying,
'Today we'll have the perfect hunt! It's all too rare, but it does
happen from time to time!' Gipsies had come to town in the
night and as usual had been arrested. His uncle was the chief
magistrate of the region and thus a law unto himself. On the
morrow at dawn they were to set off. It was only in after years
that he understood and appreciated the details about the hunt.
They had taken the gipsies the night before and among them
they had found what they wanted – a gipsy with a child at
breast! They were going to turn her loose and course her
like a stag!

"The pack was in training always, raised so to speak on
camphor and menstrual blood, for it was not always that there
was a quarry at hand during certain parts of the year. The
woman was taken off at dawn on a cart to a certain cross-
roads some miles from the village where the hunt would
begin. Her person and her clothes were dowsed with this
mixture of camphor dust and bran soaked in human menses.
They had an hour or more to take her out to the chosen point
and drop her for the hounds. Meanwhile in the manor house

all was excitement and anticipation. The little boy, cripple as he was, was taken up by the strong arms of his uncle and perched upon the high saddle from which he could command an excellent panoramic view of everything that took place. So when an hour had passed a signal was given and the horns began their deep braying sound soon to be matched by the bass baying of the great hounds which were almost as tall as the stags they had been raised to hunt. A medley of confused sounds and the whole hunt set off across the frozen marches in pursuit of the solitary cart and its victim, the woman with the suckling child.

"The cart with its two drivers dropped her at the agreed place, a point where three ways met, and with a last burst of malevolence whipped her away from the cart into the unknown. But she was a sturdy girl and hardly whimpered as she set off at a stumbling run into the snow-lit landscapes which surrounded her. There was no mistake now; she could hear the deep baying of the pack as it rolled across the marches towards her. There was no time to be lost. She must try and cross water somehow, somewhere. She ran vaguely in the direction of the river, but her memory was at fault for no river came in sight; and the baying of hounds and the shrill groans of the stag-horns thrilled her blood. She felt as if she were already bleeding to death as she ran – it was time foreshortened bleeding away in her! (I know something about that!) Then on a distant hill the hunt came into view. It made a brave show on that frosty morning, scarlet and black and bronze and gold. But she had seen water – it was not the river but a shallow estuary with several lakelets of brackish water. With luck she might save herself. The little boy shared the thrilling vision of it all with his big-boned uncle riding before him on the Spanish saddle. He saw the gipsy's bid for freedom fail. She managed to reach the water and walked into it almost to her waist, holding the child above her head. But the hounds had seen their quarry and they burst out of the woods and crashed through the thin ice-sheet of the lake in order to drag her down as they did the stags of the region. He heard her screams, and those of the little boy, and then everything was silent and the water of the estuary turned carnation-red as the hounds ate their fill. It was after all their reward for a highly successful hunt. The Master of Hounds and his whippers now drew rein and produced sustaining drinks for the hunters. The little boy was to be affected throughout his life by this scene, and not less by the enormous impression made by it upon the hunters. His uncle remained speechless and out of breath from the sexual orgasm he had experienced after witnessing the hounds at kill. And happy, tremendously elated! His laughter was the laughter of a maniac. As for the boy, he never forgot, and in every capital to which he was posted he commissioned a local artist to paint him an oil, always choosing this scene for subject. He had a whole collection of them at his home in Vienna – a whole gallery of *Gipsy Pursued by Hounds*."

Sutcliffe was quite pale with lust. "You have excited me terribly," he said in a whisper, and she replied, "Yes, I wanted to. We must make love after so long. We must fuck."

"Yes!" he almost shouted. "Yes, please, Sabine!"

She led him by the hand and they went first into a dark passage and then up a long flight of shaky stairs which led to a garret which she had borrowed from the servant. Here on a grubby bed they enacted the fulfilment of a crucial dream, recited the whole vocabulary of lust and disaffection. There was a sob buried in every kiss, as there always is when real couples meet. They pierce the thin membrane of time with every orgasm, they taste despair to the full. The partial joining of the love act was a torment – why could it not be for ever? "It's maddening! I love you irremediably!" she said, counting out his elderly heartbeats kiss by salt kiss.

They lay together later in tears of happiness, playing with each other and caressing each other with their minds. "I never thought it would happen again. I hardly recognised it the first time round! What luck!" And they thought with compassion of their poor creator who sat so stiffly over his wine now, watching the crowd flowing down to the sea, admiring the tears and the fervours and feeling sorry because he could not share them. He saw himself, Aubrey did, as a dead body lying in some furnished room in a foreign city, in a bleak hotel, made famous now because once a poet was allowed to starve to death in it! Paris, Vienna, Rome . . . what did it matter? Via Ignoto, Sharia Bint, Avenue Ignoble! Yes, Sutcliffe was right to reproach him with all the brain-wearying lumber he had taken aboard – all this soul-porridge, all this brain-mash of Hindu soul-fuck. He would change tack, he would reform. He would be possessed by a new gaiety, a new rapture. But where was Sabine?

Where indeed? She was lying in the rickety bed with her arms round her mate, staring over his shoulder at a corner of the ceiling and wondering whether this meeting would ever be repeated. She recited to herself a popular gipsy proverb. "In a lean season the gipsy never forgets that the cemeteries are full of gold teeth!" Why were they not free to forge their own futures? What damnable luck to be simply figments of the capricious human mind!

"Lovers," he said sadly, "are just reality-fools! There is nothing to be done about them!"

"And yet?"

"And yet! How good it is, how real it is!"

They embraced again violently and she said, "If you knew Spanish I would quote you the words Cervantes puts into the gipsy's mouth. It is less rich in English. Do you know them? Listen! 'Having learnt early to suffer, we suffer not at all. The cruellest torment does not make us tremble; and we shrink from no form of death, which we have learned to scorn . . . Well can we be martyrs but confessors never. We sing loaded with chains and in the deepest of dungeons. We are gipsies!' " And turning her magnificent head she made to spit twice over her right shoulder. A ritual salute. Her lover was deeply moved. He had sunk into a profound melancholy at the realisation that in a day or two they would separate once more, perhaps never to meet.

But time was getting on. A flock of horsemen galloped down the main street firing off their guns and pistols in the air, while the deep vibration of guitars was now taken up and underpinned by the skirling, pining note of mandolins – Orient answering the Occident, East mingling with West. "It's time to go!" she said, struggling back into her clothes. "I must arrange for their fortunes to be told by our tribal mother if possible. Hurry up and dress now. The party is over for us, worse luck."

The evening had started to lengthen out its shadows; they were beginning to feel footsore as they gradually found their way back to the tavern balcony which was the rallying point where the remains of their lunch still stood, waiting to be packed up in the straw hampers. But there was still wine in abundance to be disposed of, still plenty to eat . . . Therefore Cade had hesitated to start the process of packing up, for the party might go on all night. There was at least one person who hoped it would, and that was Affad's child; he had by now become quite drunk on the beauty and colour and movement. Moreover a kindly cowboy, an elderly *gardien* on a white steed, had adopted him for the afternoon at the behest of Sylvie, and he had viewed the proceedings from the crupper of a white Camargue horse, a safe enough vantage point, and one from which one could really see everything that was going on. The brilliantly dressed and painted saints, the ecstasies of the crowd, the fervour and the tremendous pulse beat of the music made him tremble with pure rapture. Never had he known anything like it. And the two women who from the depths of the crowd could see his rapture in the expression his face wore were almost as happy themselves.

By the time they had regained the balcony, however, it was to find a thoughtful Sutcliffe sitting beside Aubrey over a drink; night was slowly falling. "I have been with Sabine!" he explained. "And she has gone to try and arrange for your fortunes, though she thinks that the old girl will only accept to do three of us because it tires her so much."

As a matter of fact the witch was already drunk, though in her monumental agelessness she showed no signs of it and remained in fair coherence. She inhabited the brilliantly painted and carved caravan of the old style which was set somewhat apart from the fairground on the beach. Inside it candles and joss contended – for the wind had dropped and already the spring mosquitoes of the Camargue had started their onslaught. She was the race-mother of this small troop and everyone, even Sabine, was afraid of her; she could if she wished command the death of someone who had sinned against the ethos of the tribe – by adultery, rape or any other such trespass. Moreover she did not like or trust Sabine, whom she knew to be a woman from the world "out yonder". There was also a touch of fear, for she smelled the weight of her education, her culture. Yet Sabine was so useful that one found no excuse to gainsay her, above all when she came to propose clients who might pay well. "Shalam!" she said, twice bowing her head and pouring out another stiff portion from a bottle marked "Gin". "Shalam, Sabina! What brings you here?"

"I have clients for you. They speak English."

"Then you must stay and translate."

"I will, my mother." So they talked on for a short while; it provided an opportunity for Sabine to perform several little offices for the old lady – such as trimming the candlewicks which were burning unevenly because of the wind, and setting out the dice with which the witch literally played herself into the mood of her client, so she could "read" his preoccupations and divine their portent and shape; and also see how they would mature or fail . . . But Sabine had been right, she would not take more than three for the evening. The others might come tomorrow if they wished. And she must have half an hour alone during which time she prepared her own mind, sharpened her own faculties. A clock struck, and she said it needed winding up, an act which the younger woman performed. She agreed to transmit the message and come back with the first client within half an hour. A grunt of agreement was her only response, so she tiptoed out of the caravan and down the stairs, closing the door softly behind her.

She crossed the twilit sands towards the balcony of rendezvous bearing her message about the limitation on numbers. "Well," said Lord Galen in some dismay, "I suppose we shall have to cast lots or play at Eeni Meeni Mina Mo?" It was as logical a course as any, but they had half an hour to wrangle about it, and the final choice as a result of their deliberations fell upon Sylvie, Galen and the Prince. The others were to possess their souls in patience or submit to the ministrations of less professional seers. They did not lack for these, for as they sat at their wine the crowd threw up half a dozen cozening faces and outstretched hands of women as well as men offering a reading of hands, a guide to the future. One of the younger women was so insistent and so pretty that they adopted her and she settled like a bird of prey over the hands of Aubrey. But the language she spoke was almost unintelligible and it needed Sabine's help to decipher it. "She says you are worried about a building, a structure, something like a house which you wish to make beautiful. But it takes much writing. She is thinking of cheques and contracts – something of that order." Aubrey said, "Has she ever heard of a novel?" But there were other things also somewhat ambiguous. "Now in a little while you will have the woman of your dreams safely in your keeping, free to love you. You will know great happiness, but it will not last very long. Guard it while you have it." The advice seemed sound enough if true! But how often in the dreary routine of fortune telling must the young woman have said the same thing? As for the hand of Cade, she simply turned pale and dropped it like a hot coal. She crossed herself and spat and retreated from him with an expression of alarm. "As if she had been scalded," said Sutcliffe with amusement. "What can the poor fellow have done to frighten her?" It was not possible to find out for the girl melted away into the crowd and was replaced by a man with one eye who seemed every inch a fabricator and whom Sabine refused to encourage. She drove him off with a few sharp phrases of reproach and he left with anger and reluctance.

But with the fall of darkness new styles of celebration came into being – impromptu horse races on the sands, championships of such games as *boules*, Provençal bowling, and archery. With the Saints safely back in their niches among the *ex votos* it was time to turn to more secular amusements, so that while most of the world fell to dinner the little arenas of the village were of a sudden brilliantly floodlit and the gates thrown wide to receive their black Camargue bulls. The rest of the evening was going to be spent in bull-fighting – not the Spanish-style killing fight but the Provençal cockade-snatching ones so suitable to the temper of the place. In this mode the only danger is incurred by the white-clad fighter whose task is to snatch the cockade and skim the barrier out of reach of reprisals – for the little black bulls are fiery and carry long-horned crowns with which to defend their cockades.

Weariness was setting in, however, and it was clearly about time to start thinking of the return journey; but as yet the fortune telling was not at an end. There was nothing for it but to set the table for another repast and to replenish the glasses. This did not come amiss for some of them – notably Sutcliffe who was somewhat weary after his impromptu afternoon honeymoon. Sabine was away helping to translate the divinations of the old gipsy. The little boy had fallen asleep on a bench in a shadowy corner of the balcony, and it was clear that for him at any rate the party was over.

But when the three postulants returned with Sabine it was clear that the results had been far from satisfactory, perhaps because of the massive potations of the old lady. On the other hand both Galen and the Prince looked elated for they had been assured that the treasure they had sought so long and so ardently was a real tangible and concrete one, and not just a historic figment. But the somewhat confusional approach of the old woman had provided several enigmas, for in talking of one of them she made references to others – to Constance, for example – which were easy to decipher. But of course the usual trappings of fortune telling were present – the colourful language and imagery, for instance. Sabine's gloss went as follows: "The treasure is real and a very great one, but it is locked in a mountain and guarded by dragons who are really men. Great dangers attend the search. Nevertheless it will not be abandoned, even though the whole business could turn to tragedy. If you proceed it must be with great caution."

But despite the ambiguity Lord Galen felt a wave of optimistic elation; all the doubts and fears which had been evolving within his mind seemed set at rest. The Prince also felt elated, though of course he was less prone to believe in soothsayers. Sometimes, though . . . The reference to the mountain was tantalising, however. He shook his head doubtfully. But the person most affected by this séance was Sylvie, who returned to them step by slow step as if blasted by the weight of what she had heard. There were tears on her white face and she held her hands before her in a pleading, twisted way, as if it was their infamy which had been revealed. She had been told that her partner, companion, lover would soon leave her – indeed, that she was not any longer loved. And with this she suddenly felt the extent of her dependence upon Constance. It also clarified a lot of small incidents and occurrences – she realised that her lover was trying to find a way of breaking off their relationship, and that she was suffering with guilty feelings because of it. She was thunderstruck when she tried to imagine a world without a Constance at her side. The fearful fragility of her grasp on reality became clear – she saw herself diminishing, becoming a parody of a person, empty of all inward fruitfulness, of love. Swollen with this revelation, she felt she could hardly look her lover in the face. Drawing a shawl over her head like a gipsy in mourning she climbed back into the bus and hid herself right at the back, where soon the little boy found her and fell asleep at her side with his head in her lap. So she sat in a daze and felt the night flowing round her like the waters of a dark lake. The voices, the snarl of mandolins and the crackle of dancing heels in the main square under the portals of the church – they lacked all significance now. They referred to nothing, expressed nothing. There was no flow in things, no element of *time* to enrich the future with promises or desires. It is always at this point, when reality loses all freshness and seems unable to renew itself, that the little hobgoblin of suicide appears. Constance would have been terrified had she known of this reading entirely because of this factor. What price the psychology of the day? How untruthful it seemed, this pickpocket loving! But the one basic truth of the matter was that they must soon break up, separate from each other, rejoin the ranks of the walking

dead – those who were out of love! As the others drifted back
to their base, and thence slowly began to take their places in
the little bus, Sylvie drew her shawl closer and tried to sleep –
what a mockery! Sabine seemed somewhat anxious about her
and sat for a while with a protective arm about her shoulders
before returning to the café for a last chat with Sutcliffe.

For her part she was worried lest the idea of the impending breach might once more undermine Sylvie's fragile grasp
upon reality. "I only hope that Constance is aware of the
probabilities – but she must be because of her professional
training." Indeed Constance was when she heard of the
prophecy, and at once her affectionate compassion sent her to
the side of the girl to try to palliate the pain of the wound. In
vain, for Sylvie simply dropped her hand and said simply, "I
understand so many little things which puzzled me these last
days. You were trying to tell me that everything was over
between us." And her lover sat beside her in a sort of choked
despair, stroking the head of the sleeping boy and saying
nothing because there was nothing to say. It was clear that
out of this new information some momentous new dispositions would have to be taken. There was the danger, in a
manner of speaking, for Sylvie had nowhere to go if she
decided to leave – unless it were back to Montfavet, which in
fact was what later transpired. Constance reproached herself
bitterly for her own weakness, but it availed nothing: what
was done was done. It remained to try and skry into the future,
to the new life which so vaguely beckoned to her from beyond
the screen of the present. "No," she said, "we are friends for
ever, Sylvie!" And this too, in a strange sort of way was true.
"Don't shake your head, darling, it is true."

From the cafe's edge, where a corner of the marquee was
drawn back, Blanford watched their expressive faces with pain
and helplessness. He could not hear what they said but it was
obvious from their expressions that it was not happiness which

preoccupied them. How he longed at moments to be alone with Constance! But what could he tell her that she did not already know?

Sutcliffe, to console him and amuse Sabine, said, "When I read somewhere that Chinese peasants stuffed up the anus of their pigs with clay in order to make them weigh more when they came to market I realised in a flash why so many American novelists write to the length they do – they have been end-stopped by relentless publishers. Subject for a doctorate: 'The novelist as many-splendoured pig'." But his bondsman who was still poring upon the distant face of his true muse hardly heeded him. He sat locked into the parsimony of his sexual insight, quoting to himself the lines: "In an inferential realisation of emptiness, an emptiness is cognised conceptually or through the medium of an image. Despite the profound nature of such inferential intuition, *direct realisation* is yet to be attained!" What was one to do? But now Cade was packing up in earnest and the bus driver flashed his lights as a sign of his impending departure. They must return northward and leave the fair to dwindle away in the darkness, under a gibbous moon.

They threaded their slow way across the sands to the main road, fully aware of how many fires still burned in the darkness and how many families lay about, sleeping where they had fallen, so to speak, on a battlefield of black wine at thirteen degrees! Here and there a child still scampered across their headlamps, bent on some midnight manoeuvre. The smoky fires damped down the moonlight into spindrift which lolled and subsided upon the surface of the inland lakes – the *étangs*. But once on the more secure purchase of the macadam-ised main road, their driver turned off his gig-lamps and let the passengers swell slowly into drowsy sleep as he set sail for distant Avignon. As Blanford slept, the whirling confetti of his abandoned notes drifted him silently into a great drowsiness. He wondered what the time was because he did not wish to miss seeing the dawn come up over the river, over the spires.

But if he drowsed his bondsman did not; the events of the day had put him in a resounding good humour, not to mention the snoutful of red wine. "Ha ha, as we used to exclaim in the tropics!" he cried, banging his knee for extra emphasis. This was mysterious – why, for example, *the tropics*? But he would not have liked to be asked to explain the outburst – for him the sheerly inconsequent and the inadvertent were close to the sublime, a kingdom of mad laughter.

"Shut up!" said Aubrey, "and let me get a speck or two of sleep." But the flying confetti with its conspiratorial messages kept teasing him with its gleams of subversive insight. "Tell me, Mr B., how would you describe yourself?" Answer: "As a mortally shy man suffering from delusions of grandeur. I have been impelled to try the path of negative capability – how to cross the river without a bridge across it. I am aware that when a culture cracks up soothsayers and false witnesses abound!" All these midnight conversations with the time-clock! (If the communication between the sexes falters the whole universe, which is imaginary, is put at risk! Of course it is pure impudence to think like this.) Ah! Catspaw of the loving mind, which takes refuge in the Higher Flippancy. To sit in a cave and argue substance away dialectically could help you to shed the skin of your mind – but how laborious a method. Is there no other? Yes, there is always The Leap! The Avignon bridge symbolises it.

The real tragedy is that the whole of the Vedanta becomes mere gossip when she smiles – and nobody is to blame because the whole Universe is indifferent to our prowess!

On they went, swaying through the darkness like a night

express, only more slowly, elbowing their way through the
forests and the demesnes of divine Langue d'Oc, while
Sutcliffe informed the world at large that "human beings
displace a good deal of air – mostly hot air" and that "for
the artist to take a vow of chastity which is quintessential for
his inmost self is also to invite rape!" The lights from passing
villages briefly illumined their forms, showing who slept with
arm hunched up against the window of the coach – Cade: or
who bowed into the immensity of sorrowing sleep – Constance. Sutcliffe was humming improvisations full of the
plenitude of his genius.

> Cloud-forged and water-lulled
> From heavenly cirrus culled
> My heliocentric honey come
> Confide the treasures of thy golden bum
> To one who merits ripest sugar-plum
> Come O come!

Blanford slept and allowed the idolatrous image of his
only love gradually to overwhelm his consciousness – what
a honeycomb of smiles, what a pincushion of kisses! He
recognised this unflinching open-endedness as a way to comprehend a poetic attitude! Its theology was resolution-
proof – the religious message not penitential but exuberant.
It had its laws, the right kisses always breaking a code, the
right approach scoring points in the old-fashioned gymkhana
of self-realisation. Like the boom of surf upon the desert
lakes, his cloud of notes assailed him with both promises and
accusations. "To live in a fearless approximation to nature –
to cultivate the consciousness of material intangibility. To
create poetically in books written from the hither side of a
privileged experience – the posture of awakening. Not phrase-
making but direct experience experienced, printed and dis-
seminated. The central truth of the Dharmic brain-flash is

linguistically quite incommunicable, it outstrips language, even the most conceptual forms. It is a privileged experience. But by simply exchanging a look you can tell at once whether you share this body-snatcher's love with someone else, and the laughter follows spontaneously. The glance is not such an idle combustion of acquisitive desires but a lock-step in art of the highest reticence. You cannot help hugging yourself once you realise that there is no such thing as a self to hug! And you have all the time in the world – there is no concept of impatience in all nature!"

No escape from the dozing notebook of the brain. He told himself, "You can keep lighting candles to yourself on the great Wedding Cake of the Sages, but one day you will have to cut a slice yourself!"

Sometimes the terror of the pure meaninglessness of things seized him by the hair – for there is no reason for things to be the way they are. Suppose Aristotle to be wrong, to have wallowed in pure presumption, the observer influencing his field of observation, what then? Yet he had a feeling that the notion of emptiness would save him. Yes, to savour to the full the sheer inherence of things, so pure and gentle is it; if you get still enough you can hear the grass growing. You can see landscape in terms of a divine calligraphy! Ah, the mind-numbing ineptness of the rational man with his formulations! Defeated always by the flying multiplicity of the real. "Ordinary life" – *is* there such a thing?

Yes, the observer fouls up everything by trying to impose a plan, an intention, upon nature which can only reproduce the limitations of his understanding, the boundaries of his personal vision. He disturbs the rest of the universe which has no fixed plan, but simply lolls about and goes whichever way things tilt, just as water does. What to do then? Why, play for time just as nature does! Become what you already are! *Realise!* Discontented and vigilant body so much adored, you know too well that death and life coexist.

But as he sank deeper into his loving swoon his irrepressible bondsman took up the tale, despite the gesture of reproach sketched in the air by the Prince who wanted some peace in which to work over in his mind the prophecies they had received at the fair – for as a good Egyptian he believed in the other world of alchemy and divination. "I mean," said Sutcliffe, "how would you like to be just a counter-novelist, existing on relief on charity, or in the imagination of a friend? I wake sometimes with my face bathed in tears. Ontology-prone Judeo-Christians have stolen away my heritage. On the other hand all the gibberings of Paracelsus are coming back to us under a Tibetan imprimatur!"

"Shh!" hissed Lord Galen, wrenched from a troubled sleep by these hoarse formulations which he did not understand. "For goodness sake, let us have a tiny doze!"

"The Scythian proverb says: 'Those who eat wild garlic shall prophesy by farts!' " announced Sutcliffe gravely, though he himself was gradually being overwhelmed by the weight of sleep. To himself he went on in disconnected monologue based on the scattered notes of his maker. "If I had had a harpoon I would have thrown it – how beautiful she was! Rising from bed with the early sunlight she said, 'I must wash my eyebrows or nobody will believe me.' " The universe says nothing precise, it hints. Cade slept smiling – the smile of a dwarf preserved in pickles. Galen dreamed now of symphonic ladies with proud bums and bushes like busbies, doing yoga in groups full of cosmic munificence! A little further on were clusters of Geneva bankers practising the Primal Cry in unison, also Spontaneous Laughter on all fours. In this they were joined by dumboid damsels full of stealth conducted by *prêtres caramélisés* from the *atelier* of the head pastrycook of the town. Yet throughout it all she slept on, *jolie tête de migraine*!

It was to be an evening fecund in new departures for all of them – unexpected swerves in the action. Among them, that of Felix, who was now so rich in the munificence of his new understanding of things and people. Sylvie! He sat in the speeding coach and watched her averted face with a kind of drunken vehemence, realising with an unexpected dismay that he had fallen in love with her – it is not altogether pleasant to feel powerless and bound. He felt suddenly that he had been invented for her express wishes like a bucket for a spade! Yes, but what did she feel? There was no clue to be read in her preoccupied expressions which were all ones of stress, composed around the pain for her ruined passion and its inevitable outcome – separation. What was to become of her? For some time now this realisation had haunted him and filled him with a restlessness which he translated into physical activity. He reforged his relationship with the city which had once meant so much to him, hiring a push-bike and setting off every night after dark to traverse its squares and corners with affectionate nostalgia, recalling all the bitter privations of his consular posting, wondering how he had managed to put up with such loneliness and so many petty humiliations. Sometimes he would wind up after midnight in the little square of Montfavet and press the night bell on the wall of the asylum. The little doctor was an insomniac – he knew this of old – and hardly ever sought his bed before the first gleam of dawn light. He was always delighted by the thought of late company and would hasten to stoke up the old-fashioned olive wood fire. It was he who one day told Felix that Sylvie had sent him a message informing him of her decision to return to her old quarters in Montfavet, if he would agree to welcome her back once more. He spoke with a sorrowful resignation in which there was more than a touch of asperity which signified a criticism of Constance's role in this lamentable business. A professional criticism as between two doctors, for after all she had been in possession of all the facts and in a position to foresee all the contingencies. "It's as unexpected as it is unfair," he said, "and she should be ashamed of herself."

In fact she was, deeply ashamed, but quite powerless to act otherwise, such was the gravitational pull of her lover's charm during the first months. And now?

As for Felix, it had happened very suddenly, when he happened upon a prose poem of hers which Constance had left lying about in his room; he was startled to realise that she was far from insane, she had simply been brushed with the essential and basic illumination which comes to all virgin hearts when one bothers to prepare them. The poetic life declares itself with such force that it often looks like an alienating force which dethrones simple reason. But this isn't madness – except for behaviourists! Reality has several dialects, and the most powerful are sexual ones. The sexual code, if ignited between two people who recognise how momentous an act it is, will automatically be conducted with reserve and great timidity. "Of course," said Sutcliffe approvingly, "because the seed of all meditation is in the orgasm itself!"

But after such a realisation you cannot go on in the old way, grudging away a whole life from pure lack of attention. The sublime anguish evoked by her words had moved him to the depths, and he had "crystallised" her in his heart – that wonderful gloating walk, the whole mesmerism of her beauty. Such a profane beauty as permits almost penitence after pleasure. With each new realisation of it his passion crowded on new sail, as did his anxiety also – for if she did not respond, did not "see" him, what should he do then? Sometimes she looked so distraught that he wondered if she would refuse her jumps, or bucked so that her riders fell off. A fathomless ignorance swallowed him; he realised that you cannot codify the reality of love, for it moves too fast for the eye and mind to follow it. The sweet topic of love only dealt with a parody of the great event. Ah, to become a saint for her sake, to solicit states of calm and interventions of grace on behalf of both! Sutcliffe clicked his tongue disapprovingly and quoted one of the joke *petites annonces* of Blanford: *Druide très performant cherche belle trépannée.* To improvise on the great keyboard of love! But Sutcliffe disapproved once more and cried, "Useless! Like rubbing cold cream into the belly of a dead porcupine." Until death do us nudge into the total reticence; man's function on earth is to allow it to realise itself in him. Ugh! But once you stop caring in the wrong (i.e. awkward) way, everything starts to cooperate and blitheness sets in and the lovers comprehend everything. Felix appeared in her room and wildly, impulsively, said to her as he took her hands, "Sylvie, don't let them send you mad again – let me love you! Your illness is just the growing pains of a solitary cogniser. In Japan they would give a party to celebrate the vision you have experienced! It is the first step by which the yogi gains admittance to his final omniscience! I want to marry you and look after you otherwise you will stop writing out of fear like Rimbaud! Come and live with me."

Yet as she trembled in amazement and hesitated before slowly toppling into his embrace, Constance by the same token was bitterly addressing the mirror image of herself: "You cannot be a doctor and a human being at one and the same time!"

On they travelled through darkness stained with patches of white, the noise of their springs creating around the dozing forms echoes of a secret language – voices repeating obsessive phrases over and over again, like "miniature pigeons", "miniature pigeons" or else "conscientious gypsum" over and over. Blanford listened in his sleep, reminded of older hallucinations. He reminded his other that "when Professor Dobson began to break up he started reacting with dismay to the conversation of French intellectuals, specially men with bushy beards. If any such person cleared his throat and started a sentence with *'C'est évident que la seule chose . . .'* or else *'Je suis tout à fait convaincu que . . .'* he turned pale and faint with distress and if nothing were done he fell slowly to the ground, to lie there helplessly drumming his heels."

"I don't know how you can talk after undertaking this weird prose barbecue, evolving a vexatious prose style based on Rozanov, Hegel's *Aesthetics* and Mallarmé's *Igitur*."

This for some reason irritated Blanford who felt forced into a defence of his methods. "Nonsense. I have been explicit enough to expose my thoughts most clearly. My style may be described as one of jump-cutting as with cinema film. The basic illustration is of course the admission that reincarnation is a fact. The old stable outlines of the dear old linear novel have been sidestepped in favour of soft focus palimpsest which enables the actors to turn into each other, to melt into each other's inner lifespace if they wish. Everything and everyone comes closer and closer together, moving towards the one. The great human models – the Emperors and Empresses – were related by blood ties, were brothers married to sisters. Breath by breath, stitch by stitch, they wove their winding sheet of kisses and prayers. Even before puberty she was there in my bed, the little tantric mouse. Their speech became a rainbow. After them came poets to live in a bewilderment of women. But the book, my book, proved to be a guide to the human heart, whose basic method is to loiter with intent, in the magic phrase of Scotland Yard, until the illumination dawns! The apparent disorder is only superficial and is due to the fact that part of the notes which I scattered out of the train window were notes I had borrowed with permission from Affad – the little sermons he pronounced at Macabru in the desert. Huge bundles of them were stored in the muniments room at Verfeuille. They were full of striking gnostic aphorisms and I copied many into my own notebooks. Hence the overlap.

"By the same token the people also, and even pieces of them, spare parts which are not as yet fully reincarnated. One must advance to the edge of the Provisional, to the very precipice! And when you think of it, you haven't done too badly considering that you are only a figment of my fancy; you could be considered as more than half Toby when it comes to the novel which I almost wrote and then funked because of all these considerations. Somehow you have managed to hold your separateness, your own identity . . . do I mean that? Yes, a book like any other book, but the recipe is unusual, that is all. Listen, the pretension is one of pure phenomenology. The basic tale which I have passed through all this arrangement of lighting is no more esoteric than an old detective story. The distortions and evocations are thrown in to ask a few basic questions like – how real is reality, and if so why so? Has poetry, then, no right to exist?"

Dawn was breaking with its chaste silver points of lake and forest, and their sleep entered a deeper and sweeter register; reality seemed fragile, provisional – a mere breath might blow it out like a candle, so you felt. Indeed, the snoozing Blanford who dwelt among dreams which seemed felicitous abbreviations of truth, told himself that a human being might be described as simply a link between two breaths. Oblong thoughts to drive philosophers like Quine and Frege sane, again! To siphon off love, to hive off desire, that fancy reptile by what Sutcliffe called "low grade mercy-fucking by some inadequate pixie – someone with big elementary toe-nails and salient balls!"

Memory dropping stitches; all night long in his sub-conscious played a sleek and baleful jazz – *esprit de vieux piano-bar! Le baisodrome vétuste de l'âme française!* It is not as Cioran has it *"de bricoler dans l'incurable"*, but rather "*bricoler dans l'incroyable*" once the vision makes itself felt. In the terms of the true alchemy both worldliness and vanity can be seen through and defeated by countermeasures. You need not give in to media clowns or dozing quietists. (I wish you would shut up and let me sleep.) I am six foot of pink convinced English baby and I write prose without thrust. Cade, go bring me my love-bacon, my sex-grog!

But Cade's dark nightmares were of a uniform scheme and content – picture of a huge insect as the World, using primitive factors of intelligence which worked functionally but which were devoid of affectivity, of feeling! Poor fellow, this was troubling; but nevertheless he felt himself to be the servant of this faculty. Rather like someone who finds that he can read minds unerringly. It makes him feel always a little apologetic. To see so far . . .

The World as an armour-plated saurian with an insect mind and belated feathers – the mindlessness condemned by the gnostics, but which ruled the world. The Beast! What could be done to replace such a monster by something a little more human? Apparently nothing whatsoever.

In the case of Constance the situation with Sylvie led to a breach with the little doctor who had loved her so devotedly for more than a decade. He burst out: "What a fearful aberration this has been! How could you give in to such a folly – and drag this mad girl back once more into schizophrenia and quite possibly suicide? Constance! I am angry with you because you know better. You are not Livia with her *partie à trois*! It has been an amazing folly." Constance was on the point of bursting into tears but she resisted the feeling and said, "I *fled* into this parody of passion to defend myself against the realisation of Affad's piteous death – I felt it would drive me insane. I hid like this and played for time until I could muster the courage to confront the hole in the middle of nature which he left me!" He turned his back to hide his emotion and she realised how much she meant to him. "We don't have any luck as far as love is concerned!" she went on with bitterness, "and I was rather counting on your sympathy. It hurts to be reproached."

Nevertheless he was right and she knew it. But in order not to wound her too irremediably he changed the subject of the conversation in the direction of Livia. "You tell me that you are still asking questions about Livia. But did you know that several Germans who might know something about her are still with us? No? Well, Smirgel the double spy is still in Avignon. He was able to demonstrate quite triumphantly that he was working for the British all the time with his own transmitter. But more astonishing still is the existence of Von Esslin, the German general who commanded here. He is almost blind owing to an accident and has been more or less hospitalised in the Nîmes Eye Clinic while he awaits trial on a War Crimes charge of one sort or another. There must be others around but these two are likely to be able to help, and in the case of old Smirgel they were actually associates, were they not? I mean that the two worked together up at the fortress. I have got his address in my day book since he often comes round to read to depressive patients – he enjoys doing that. So you could ring him and make a rendezvous if you wished to ask him questions about Livia . . ."

How extraordinary to realise that these relics from the war were still in existence, and still in Provence! It seemed hardly possible, so far away did the war seem with all its follies. "The General!" she thought. "Perhaps it would be worth it!"

Yes, she would visit him.

FOUR

The General Visited

FOR A SHORT WHILE NOTHING WAS TO COME OF THESE notions, but then with the first few warm days of spring they gradually took shape and turned into promptings fed by her native impatience and the impending changes in their lives – for Blanford had decided that if Sylvie betook herself off to her old quarters in Montfavet he himself might return to Tu Duc at last. Constance seemed to favour the idea at any rate. So she found her thoughts turning in the direction of old Von Esslin who spent his days cooped up in the little Eye Clinic of Nîmes in a state of ambiguous half-imprisonment, waiting upon a War Crimes Tribunal to pronounce on his dossier. He was almost blind and the prognosis for the future was so poor that he had already invested in the traditional white cane, though in fact he could just dimly see things and people, often only as outlines which he filled in from memory. He sat stiffly at a child's desk trying to learn a little elementary French in order to temper his isolation and loneliness. The authorities treated him with respectful civility proper to his exalted rank and this did not surprise him for, as he was to put it to Constance, "They understand the logic of the uniform – what is a crime after all? A soldier's duty comes first and they know it." It was one of those intellectual quibbles which left a bad taste in the mouth, like the scholar's proposition that "The Templars were the bankers of God but not of Christ"!

Things did not move with great urgency, nor were the French anxious to hasten them, for with every new move the full extent of their shameful collaboration with the Germans became more and more clear. As for Von Esslin he felt rather an orphan for he had lost touch with his family and home which was occupied by Russian troops now. What little news that leaked out was anything but reassuring. Later on he would find out that the Russian Army, responding to reports of Nazi atrocities further East, had burned the chateau. His mother and sister had perished, locked in a barn with the servants. The silence emphasised his isolation. The world had closed in and his movements were limited to a walk of a few hundred yards in the romantic public gardens of that austere fief of Protestantism, the city of Nîmes. He tapped his way across them until he found a sunny spot in which to sit, basking in sunlight whenever there was any, like an old lizard. He suffered very much from the winter cold, for the little clinic was inadequately heated.

It was of course a great surprise when Constance burst into his life as she did, without warning, and she supposed that it was the surprise of her perfect German which made him disposed to welcome her. But in fact it went deeper, very much deeper than she herself would ever guess, for through the screens of his fading vision the blonde and beautiful woman seemed to be reincarnating a screen-memory of his blonde sister Constanza – even to the name! "My name is Constance," said Constanza, and a piteous pang of joyful recognition was his first reaction. Of course confusion and disappointment followed it – he had wondered for a wild moment whether by some miraculous military dispensation the real Constanza had not been permitted by the Red Cross to cross the lines and visit him . . . It was cruel, and it took some time to accommodate himself to the truth. It was also in a way exasperating, for this life-inspiring vision had to be continuously edited and re-edited to meet the needs of the present. Moreover the sweet resemblance of voice together with her mannered stylish Prussian turns of speech went far to confirm at first blush that it actually *was*, it might be, it could be, *must* be his sister! Alas! But in their first interview while the girl introduced herself and opened up the subject of it, this thirsty delusion came down over his heart and mind like manna from heaven and it was little wonder that within an hour he was devotedly at her service and fully ready to cooperate with her in her quest for more information about Livia. His age and fragility were touching. They became friends.

What seemed strange at first was the fact that they remembered nothing of each other despite the fact of having spent so long together in the same city during the same critical period. Perhaps twice she had seen him with a column of soldiers crossing the town, face turned away, pale and remote as a cipher – which is what he was. He could not remember having seen her at all, otherwise he must have been struck by the resemblance to his sister. Of Livia he knew only a little and that by accident, for he had spent a weekend in the infirmary of the fortress being nursed for an infected tooth, and this rather taciturn field nurse was on duty that week. But the eminence of his rank had hardly encouraged them to indulge in casual conversation. Nevertheless he had heard some vague gossip about the English girl who had defaulted to join the Nazis and who was working as a staff nurse in the field force. He himself felt that such independence merited admiration and was rather shocked when the security officer who outlined her record spoke of her with pity and contempt. They were suspicious of Livia apparently, and in part it was due to her association with Smirgel who was the senior intelligence officer posted in Avignon and whose acquaintance with her dated from before the war when he had been an art student spending a period of study in the town on a scholarship. He had met Livia one day while working on the restoration of a painting and they had, with some hesitation, become lovers.

"So much I learned, I overheard, so to speak. But I gave the matter no thought as we had so much already on our hands. Nevertheless I often heard doubts about Smirgel's reliability expressed, specially because he had accepted a working brief with the English, but only in order to mislead or betray them – or at any rate this is what he said. It could have been true – why not? But in a war rumour runs wild, and nobody believes anybody else. At any rate the old field reports must exist somewhere unless the French went ahead and had them destroyed to avoid causing themselves much unnecessary soul-searching because of the past. One can understand it. They were more zealous than us all when it came to hunting down the dissenters. In my own view there would have been no real resistance at all after the first few months had we not gone ahead with our slave-labour policy. That is what set up a wave of reaction and got people evading the draft and taking to the hills. Once that started the British started parachuting in and forming an armed resistance among these runaway slaves; and of course the terrain around LaSalle and in the fastnesses of Langue d'Oc favoured such a development."

He shook his head with an expression of regret and went on: "And what complicated matters was the three overlapping intelligence agencies, often with conflicting tales to tell about the same incidents. My own role was purely military though I had access to all. I depended on the field command and had an intelligence group of my own, dealing only with that. Then came the military governor who had his own security service which he shared with the French Milice – which he loathed and distrusted, though he managed to foist most of the dirty jobs on to them. Nor did they mind. They seemed to take pleasure in roughing up their own nationals. That is why they are in such a state now, for so many animosities were created, and the Frenchman harbours grudges, he does not forgive and forget!"

He had been drawing in the gravel with his cane – a sketch of the interlapping agencies; now he tapped once or twice as he added, "You see? While nominally working together we were very much divided internally. Nobody could stand the Milice and the dislike was reciprocated for the Milice had a bad conscience. That is why they have pounced on the documents in the case. As far as I am concerned I am convinced that not a scrap of paper will emerge from it all. The dossiers are too incriminating for them. You mark my words, it will all be destroyed and a new race of war heroes will emerge from the ashes. French propaganda is very astute and they must prove they did something in order to give themselves bargaining power when it comes to the negotiations of the peace table. I think so at any rate! But then they would say I was prejudiced against them."

He sighed and shook his head in a sad, reproachful way. So the conversation ran on in somewhat haphazard fashion: it was so intoxicating to speak his own tongue again that it was almost unmanning for the soldier in him – he felt almost tearful with gratitude. Moreover to speak to this shadow-lambent version of his own beloved Constanza . . . waves of sympathy passed over his old heart like wind flowing over embers he had long thought cold. He even dared to reach out and touch her hand which did not withdraw from the contact but stayed for a calm moment unstirring in his. It fired his thoughts, this warm contact, though he had little enough to recount about Livia. No, it was obvious that she would have to try to trace Smirgel. She told him how some time late in the war – indeed, just before the general retreat – Smirgel had visited her to ask her opinion about a document which he had procured which purported to be an order of the day signed by Churchill himself. It was an optimistic evaluation of the war situation saying that the Germans had begun to stockpile in back areas and must now be considered as having gone over on to the defensive. Smirgel wanted to know whether she thought it a fake or not. Later when she thought over the episode she thought that it had been a clumsy attempt to worm his way into her confidence. But *why*?

The General provided an excited comment of corroboration to this by saying: "Good Lord! Yes! I well recall that English document with its message. It was very striking because it happened to be true. We had already started anticipating a defensive battle or two in the south of France – to consolidate the Mediterranean axis, for Italy had begun to defect and disintegrate. But even more than that I can tell you that when the Allied radio piously announced that no historical or archaeological treasures would be bombed it gave us at once a clue as to what should be done with all this precious stockpile of weaponry which was pouring into France by rail, road and water! We would mask it if possible by placing it in sites to be spared aerial attack. What better, for example, than to hollow out the quarries and caverns which abut the Pont du Gard? It was a God-given site. The kilometres of subterranean corridors and caves were ideal for the purpose. So we directed our sappers to perform and so they did. And the quantity grew and grew."

He had grown visibly rather tired and his exposition had begun to flag somewhat. But he did not wish this delicious exchange to end and he quested about in his mind to find an excuse to bring her back again. "It is time for my medicine soon," he said with regret at last. "But perhaps I will remember other matters of interest later on; would you wish us to meet again for a talk next week?" To his surprised relief she said yes. She found his obvious regret at parting from her touching. "Yes, we should meet again," she said, "just in case we have overlooked some detail or other which might help me. And next week you can pick your day because I am on leave for a few days." He was delighted and shook hands warmly as they parted.

So it was that this initial contact flowered into a series of short agreeable visits to the old man which enabled her to relive and re-experience those sad and barren war years spent in echoing Avignon. Nor were the visits valueless from the point of view of information, for many a small detail about life at that obscure epoch awoke under the stimulus of her company. Apart from this, too, she was able to secure for him certain small concessions and attentions on the part of the clinic, such as a cigarette and wine allowance – he was after all a prisoner of war and should enjoy certain entitlements due to his rank. And while the season advanced towards the more clement end of the spring she tried to assemble and collate these tiny fragments of history for her own satisfaction. At first Jourdain proved somewhat cold and hostile towards her acceptance of Sylvie's leave-taking but later when he sensed the full extent of her regrets he changed back into his former generous self, though when he heard that Blanford had decided to return to Tu Duc he could not repress a jealous pang. He knew nevertheless that Constance had decided that she would herself undertake the extensive physiotherapy which was part of the treatment for the rehabilitation of Blanford's wounded back which had vastly improved under her care. But one of the more surprising new elements which emerged from the General's recollections concerned the vast cache of arms which had been stored in the caverns and corridors of the Roman quarries of Vers and elsewhere. The regiment of sappers charged with the task of storing all this weaponry was Austrian and had ended by openly mutinying and refusing to blow up the train full of ammunition which the Nazi command had planted on the bridge over the river which commanded the town. (Had they obeyed the command they would have irremediably disfigured, indeed completely destroyed, Avignon.) The Austrian refusal saved the town, but the sappers themselves, all twenty of them, had been arrested and unceremoniously shot. The grateful townsfolk had covered their graves with roses when the army at last abandoned the town and started to retreat northward ... So much was mere history. But the work of the sappers had given rise to strange rumours about discoveries made while they were burrowing their way under the Pont du Gard, clearing out the debris of ancient excavations to make room for their stockpile.

They claimed – at least the two officers commanding the operation – that their men had stumbled upon an oaken door set in the rock in the very heart of the labyrinth – a steel-studded door which when forced opened upon a small nest of caves of a beehive pattern. These were of fine workmanship, the walls carefully rendered to secure the place against damp. These nooks were positively crammed with treasure, all the crates carefully assembled and tidily disposed. Their astonished eyes took in not only gold bars and coin but also a small mountain of precious stones and other specie, while a Latin wall inscription gave them to understand that the hoard was of Templar provenance! Templar! At first there was some confusion and a good deal of scepticism, for the lieutenant in charge of the Austrians was a renowned liar and drunkard. Moreover he intimated that in order to safeguard their find they had carefully mined and booby-trapped the corridors which surrounded the entry to the principal cave with its door set in the rock, and that it would be perilous to attempt to visit the site without a detailed map of the booby-traps, not least because of the fear of setting off the explosive stored all round – the original stockpile which occupied the surround of caverns and corridors! If there was at first some disposition to disbelieve the contentions of the Austrian lieutenant, his story was given substance and force by the fact that he and his fellow-soldier were both able to produce some precious stones which they alleged they had abstracted from one of the great oaken chests, before shutting the place up and wiring up the surrounding caves with defensive explosives.

What irony! So thought Constance when she learned of these developments. "The Templar treasure, though at long last discovered, remains as always obstinately out of reach due to the freakish developments of a new war." She smiled ruefully for she could see in her mind's eye the expressions which would flit like bats across Lord Galen's face – hunger, elation, fear, vexation, if ever she got to tell him the astonishing story, as she supposed she one day must – foiled again! And yet . . . surely there *must* have been a map at some time, if only to enable the Austrian discoverers of the place to gain access to it once more? Somewhere, somebody must have kept a record of the booby-trappings. But all the sappers were dead, executed by the Nazis for the crime of refusing to destroy the city! And who would risk treasure-hunting in this vast stockpile of ammunition? How maddening all these contingencies were! The old soldier was all sympathy for her exasperation; yet when she told him of her excursion to the Saintes Maries and of the gipsy pronouncements upon the treasure – namely, that it was real enough but guarded by dragons – he chuckled and struck his knee with his palm, saying: "One strange thing – the Austrian sappers had been formed from a disbanded regiment of Imperial dragoons and were entitled to wear a dragon on their shoulder-flash in memory of their origins. There you have your so-called 'dragons' if you wish to interpret the prophesy like that!" It was highly plausible to a superstitious mind and she could just see the Prince lapping it up with delight. But of course the principal dilemma remained – namely, what if anything could be done about the treasure hoard? Presumably nothing in default of further information. "I see that you are vexed and disappointed," said old Von Esslin with compassion, for familiarity had done nothing to quell the ardour of his admiration for Constance, "and I quite understand. I will have a further think about the matter and see whether any solution could present itself. But of course it would be madness just to wander about in the *cache* without knowing what one was doing. This group of active mutineers were not joking. They meant business and they knew their jobs."

For a while it seemed that the whole subject had reached a stalemate and that no further advance was to be expected. Then there was a diversion which was provided by the sudden appearance of the doctor, Jourdain, at Tu Duc one middle-morning, riding a bicycle, and bringing news of the reappearance on the scene of Smirgel, the wartime double agent who had so much occupied their thoughts. "He has re-emerged from hiding to provide evidence before a war crimes tribunal about criminal activities during the last days of the occupation. He is in quite a state, as you can imagine, and is trying to save his skin and his name by betraying a number of his erstwhile colleagues! At least so it looks to me. He is an incorrigible fellow, and a liar of the first order. I have a sort of unwilling admiration for him as a specimen. From the medical point of view he astonishes me by remaining just this side of a fine full efflorescent paranoia. I wonder how he does it." Aubrey Blanford, who was listening and playing a hand of solitaire with himself, said, "Perhaps he should be writing novels?" and Jourdain smiled. He went on: "At any rate with a matching effrontery he dropped in on me for a drink and tried to sound me out as a possible witness in his favour – a role I carefully sidestepped, as I don't know what he was up to during the occupation, how should I? But I told him that you, Constance, were trying to locate him, hoping to question him in your private capacity about Livia and her mysterious activities. This seemed to make him startled and a bit distrustful. He seemed somewhat unwilling to be met again – I feared he would disappear – but after I had talked to him for a while he calmed down and listened attentively. I stressed that you would be a valuable ally for him in case of trouble with investigating tribunals and it might be worth his while to humour your request. So suddenly he gave in and said that he would meet you on condition that only you knew of the place of rendezvous. He proposes this afternoon at four – hence my appearance all of a sudden here. I bring a letter with the details."

He extracted the sealed envelope from his pocket and placed it in the hand of Constance saying, "Ouf! I am rather out of breath with all this activity, but I have done my duty. What about treating me to a glass of wine before I take myself off? It would be an act of kindness . . ." They hastened to comply with his request and the three of them sat on for a while on the terrace, in the shade of the apple trees, while Constance with a mixture of curiosity and elation opened her envelope and started to read her message, written in the spidery hand of the evasive Smirgel. It was written in German – so he had not forgotten! "Dear Madam, I understand from our mutual friend, the good doctor Jourdain, that you wish to see me. I would be glad to comply with this wish and ask you to accept a rendezvous which, owing to my present activities and preoccupations, seems suitable, as I am not entirely my own master and am very busy. Therefore I will wait for you between four and five tomorrow at the Montfavet Church which of course you know so well. I will sit in the fifth side chapel. I trust this is acceptable to you. Yours Sincerely." The signature was a squiggle. She replaced the letter in the envelope and thanked Jourdain for his good offices. They had decided in the course of these exchanges to keep him for lunch, and from the kitchen came the agreeable clatter of pans and pots.

So it was that with a westering sunlight she took her little car along the familiar roads towards the city; Jourdain sat beside her for she had persuaded him to double his bicycle into the back of her little car, folding it up as far as possible, so to speak. She dropped him first and then drove back into the shady little square with its quiet tenantry of olive trees and cypresses. She parked it against the wall in the shade and switched off the motor to sit for a moment recalling her last weird meeting with Livia in this pleasant precinct so many years ago. She recalled the precise tone in which she had said the words "I have lost an eye!"; and how she had all the time kept her face turned away from her sister, as if ashamed of the deformity. How had she lost an eye? Ruminating upon these forgotten events she slowly crossed the sunlit-dappled grove and entered the quiet church, now deserted and shadowy, to find herself at last in the side chapel under the oil-painted witnesses, so gauche and awkward. On the wall at her back was a plaque with an inscription commemorating the death of some now forgotten priest.

ICI REPOSE

PLACIDE BRUNO VALAYER

Evêque de Verdun

Mort en Avignon

en 1850

The painting was of a poor style, a poor period. And how wan, abstracted and faraway were the faces of the three presiding over this silent edifice. Yet not entirely silent, for somewhere outside among green leaves and bowers of shade a nightingale stammered out a phrase and then was suddenly silent, as if it had grown abashed. Well, she had arrived a few minutes early, so it was too soon to become anxious about the arrival of Smirgel. She closed her eyes for a moment, the better to dream of the past in this rich corner of silence with its opaque afternoon light – a place for guided loneliness across the breathing silences and the one-pointed plains of deliberate unreason towards the mystical nudge which might set the dreamer off on a new trajectory towards the light! Towards a new objective – to try and make death fully conscious of itself! In the midst of these lucubrations she found herself falling asleep in the pew she sat in, and it was with something of a start that she woke at last to find that Smirgel had succeeded in entering the little church noiselessly and sat in the pew beside her, looking smilingly at her sleeping face. She was a little bit put out of countenance as she tried to muster her questions. "Of course it must be you," she said, to which he replied, "Have I changed so very much, then?" In truth he had. He had become extremely thin and now dressed shabbily enough, while his hair had been cropped rather short – it was fairly grey. But the old deviousness and invincibility of spirit still shone in his eyes; they had narrowed with cunning and he was saying, "I have no idea what I can tell you that you don't know, but I will do my best to meet with your demands. But will you in return help me if I need help one of these days? I suppose that Jourdain told you that I am being called before a war tribunal to answer for so-called criminal activities just before the collapse, our collapse. The truth of the matter is that I was working for the British on the promise that they would take the fact into account after the war. But now on the plea that I was a double agent working for my own side they claim that they owe me nothing for such work! Can you beat it?" He sat back in his pew and shook his head self-commiseratingly. Constance felt it was wise not to allow any strings to be attached to the transaction and said, "I can't make any promises, I am afraid – otherwise we can go no further. I cannot pose conditions myself either. I was just curious to find out something more about my sister Livia and her strange and tragic ending. At that time you seemed to know a good deal about her, but I refrained from asking you anything. It might not have been felt suitable while war conditions were such as they were. But now that things are changing back to peacetime conditions I thought I might try once more. Do you see?"

"Ah! Livia!" he said, sighing deeply. "Who will ever find out the truth about Livia?" Was it an illusion or did he swallow a lump of chagrin as he spoke? It was as if the thought of Livia came suddenly upon him, without warning, to drown him in the toils of an unrequited desire and memory. She found herself watching him curiously to study the sorrowful lines which these thoughts hatched upon that deceitful countenance. He was thinking deeply, painfully – perhaps re-creating her image with its wounded eye. He said gruffly, "Of course it is useless to tell you how much one could care for such a girl – you know that only too well! But in my case memory goes back beyond the war to when I first met her. We were both much much younger, and I did not know you or your family or your home. I was a German student of archaeology, specialised in the restoration of historic objects – paintings, pottery, glass and so on. The Society had sent me to Avignon to help restore its most famous painting. I was young and ardent, a keen National Socialist as we all were then. To my surprise so was she. You cannot realise what it meant to have someone English approving of one's political direction – it filled one with relief and happiness. Moreover a girl, a beautiful one. I could not help but love such a person. I became a slave to Livia. We met every day before the great painting. She held my brushes and paints for me. Her patience was exemplary. But sometimes she disappeared from view for several days, though she would never say where she had been. For a while after we became lovers I was wildly happy and then a kind of doubt began to seep in. It was as if inside herself, deep down, she enjoyed a profound reserve which prevented her from really giving herself in love. It was as if in her heart she were listening to faraway music or voices; they gave her a kind of dreamy detachment, of abstraction which left her lover baffled and somehow unsatisfied despite the passion they exchanged. I felt cheated and sometimes proposed to break off the affair, but she pleaded with me not to – pleaded with intensity and force that convinced me to stay on as her humble servant. I realised that I loved the girl, but that she did not love me in the same way, or in the same degree. I wondered why. Then, during one of her disappearances, I had a chance to see some new sides to her character, for one of the gipsies came to me and said that I should go to her as she had fallen ill – from smoking *quat*, he said. He led me to a corner of the town near 'les Balances': and there, on the third floor of a dilapidated house which was most likely a bordello, I found Livia, deadly sick in bed, just as the gipsy had indicated. The reasons were evident also. I was alarmed and debated whether to call a doctor or not. But at last I decided to get her home first, to my lodgings which were respectable enough, before calling in a doctor."

He paused to light a cigarette and she was intrigued to see how much his fingers trembled as he did so; by contrast the tone of his recital was dry, monotonous and without emphasis. But the expression on his face remained withdrawn, almost deceitful in its deliberate expressionlessness. After a brief hesitation – as if he was not quite sure in which order he should present the facts of his story – he went on with a trifle more animation. "The gipsy had a two-wheeler, a barrow on which he exposed his wares for sale, mostly old clothes. I persuaded him to help me place the sleeping form of Livia on it and cover it with clothes and blankets. At break of day nobody noticed us wheeling her through the silent streets to my own lodgings where we managed to get her up to my rooms and into the comfortable bed, while I talked the land-lady into sanctioning the new visitor who had, as I told her, fallen ill of a stomach ailment due to the highly spiced food: a common enough event. I had built up a reputation for seriousness and studious application to my books, so everything was all right. The young doctor whom the landlady summoned was also discreet and pleasant and I was able to confide fully in him, which was a relief. So Livia hovered for a week or so between sleep and waking while we fed and protected her. But for long periods during this time she lived in a state of hallucination, she had visions; this is how I made some new discoveries, unpleasant ones, about her past. Because of her state of mind she was off her guard and confided in me things which perhaps in her ordinary state she would not have wanted known. That is how I discovered about Hilary, her brother . . ."

He jumped to his feet now in some agitation for he had also discovered that it was somewhat inappropriate to smoke cigarettes in the chapel and he walked to the portal in order to throw the stub of his cigarette outside. "Hilary!" she echoed in some confusion, standing up herself in order to let him pass her. "What has Hilary got to do with all this?" He looked at her keenly under depressed eyebrows as if her surprise astonished him – as if she should have been quite *au courant* with what he was about to reveal. Having despatched his cigarette stub he turned and returned to her side, motioning her to sit down once more. It was as if he said, "Pray sit down, because I have a lot more to reveal to you." And obediently she sat down again under the oil-painting, but feeling now a sort of anxiety take possession of her. And Hilary, so long absent from her thoughts, now suddenly became a figure of significance and colour. He had been killed on active service with the Intelligence Corps; she had heard vaguely that he had been parachuted into France to help the Resistance, and captured by the Germans. That was all.

"Hilary, my brother," she said quietly, "was in the

process of taking Holy Orders when the war broke out. He felt sufficiently strongly about it to adopt a pacifist stance, and retire to his Scottish monastery, breaking off all contact with the rest of us – the order he joined was a silent order, so this was understandable. He kept this up for some years until gradually his intellectual posture changed, became modified. He joined the Intelligence Corps and offered to serve abroad with the Resistance; he was actually sent to France, but captured by the enemy and executed. *Voilà*! That is all I know. As a matter of fact I didn't ask for more details – once he was dead, what did further details matter?"

"I hope what I am about to tell you won't be unwelcome or shocking, but I wish to explain why I hated Hilary so profoundly. It was because of Liv. I don't suppose that it was the first time in history that a brother seduced his sister sexually – but unhappily it affected me. I realised from what she revealed to me that in fact Hilary was responsible for shaking her affective stability with this unlucky passion which neither could renounce. To do him justice he often lamented their fate, often tried to unshackle himself from his sister, make a desultory move or two in the direction of freedom, or of other women. But in vain. I realised now that he was really the author of my misfortune, that Liv would never come right, be cured, so long as the magnet of Hilary's presence existed somewhere in the world. All other relations were worthless to her while her brother lived and breathed. It was terrible, but the realisation of this fact poisoned my waking life. I was filled with vengeful thoughts, and indeed at long last, and quite by chance, fate made it possible to execute them."

She must have looked astonished or perhaps even dismayed, for he broke off suddenly and gazed anxiously at her as he said, "May I go on, please? I do not wish to shock or hurt you but I feel the need to explain many of my actions in the light of this overriding passion of Liv's; if possible, to excuse my own actions."

"Of course," she said, a prey now to old memories which welled up in her mind. They took on another light in view of these facts – new shafts of light struck them and forced her to re-evaluate them! "Of course," she said, "by all means let us have the truth, since we have all suffered so much from it."

He cleared his throat and resumed his painful narrative – it obviously cost him something after all to reveal these things.

"As for me, I followed much the same sort of trajectory in my own thinking – it took a few years but at long last I too grew disillusioned with the Nazis and ashamed of my own passivity in the face of Nazi doctrines and Nazi acts. I began to search for ways and means to escape the collapse I could see coming to meet us. I thought I might perhaps offer my services to the British. But how to make contact with them? One had to take a risk. I wrote a frank letter to the BBC which I entrusted – it was extremely foolhardy – to someone with a neutral passport who was going to Africa. Then I waited in a state of great anxiety in case the letter had been found, had been confiscated . . . But then one day I received a communication from a post office box in Avignon which gradually materialised, so to speak, into the person of a young French woman who ran a group of patriot agents and through whom I managed to inherit a transmitter and a code with a wavelength call-number which put me in direct touch with London, which is what I wanted. Of course it took me a little while to establish my *bona fides* but at last I did – it will seem ironic to you, but while neither side fully believed in my honesty both were exultant at having penetrated the enemy intelligence service. This was due to the selection of information titbits which I revealed, first to one side and then to the other.

Paradoxically both were soon content to accept my double agency, knowing that I could also pass false information to mislead the enemy! Indeed I was already operating a successful double option when I came to see you with that rather puzzling text which you may or may not remember. It was quite genuine, I discovered later. Secretly I was hoping that we might strike a chord of sympathy and make a sincere contact which would enable us to talk, but you proved too suspicious to offer me any encouragement and I felt unable to confide anything in you for the time, though of course the whole situation as well as the tragic dénouement weighed very heavily on me – as you may well imagine."

For a while now he fell silent and looked full of self-reproach, fingering his chin as if debating within himself whether to go on or not. He had turned quite pale as well. He shook his head doggedly and suddenly blurted out, "It isn't easy to say, but I mustn't disguise from you that fact that I am responsible for your brother Hilary's death – and in a secondary way for Livia's also." He hung his narrow head – it was as if the full weight of what he had said were now suddenly made manifest to him: as if he had difficulty in assimilating its significance. He stared at her with the face of a sick vulture and lapsed into silence, weighed down it would seem by an immense depression and sadness.

Surprise bereft her of speech, deprived her of any capacity to react appropriately to this surprising and shocking piece of information; and with the surprise came a twinge of doubt as to its veracity. With Smirgel one was always being overshadowed by the angel of doubt. One was condemned to wonder what hidden motives might lie hidden behind the words he uttered. If all this were a tissue of falsehood, for example, why tell her, Constance, about it: why reopen the subject which was obviously as painful to him as to her? Nevertheless, "Go on!" she said, as if admonishing him for his lack of courage to continue. This soon resulted in him rising to his feet and starting to pace up and down the narrow causeway between the pews of the little chapel with his hands behind his back, gathering together the threads of his slow narrative.

"As you will imagine, much of my work was concerned with the Resistance which had slowly started to become a reality, a possibility, owing to the insane slave-labour policy of the Reich which drove the young people to take refuge in the hills to escape conscription in the slave battalions. Soon almost every hideout in the Cévennes was full of shirkers. They had nothing to eat, of course, and arms drops alternated with food drops as they were slowly transformed into military formations. A few I actually betrayed to my own people in order to keep my reputation for truth, but the most not. The heavily wooded country round LaSalle and Durfort were the obvious places for such activities – the real mountains begin around there – and despite frequent military sweeps by our troops and the Vichy police it was seldom that the guerillas were surprised. But of course the whole question was eagerly debated by both London and Marseilles, and all the time people were coming through to evaluate the importance of such movements. Agents were parachuted into the Cévennes in gradually increasingly doses. Of course I kept a sharp eye on all this activity, and by now London trusted me implicitly with a good deal of secret information which sometimes I revealed to my own people for obvious reasons. Then one day I got some queries from London which made me prick up my ears. They had got wind of the fact that Livia was serving in the Army unit which was doing garrison duty in Avignon. Don't ask me how. But someone was trying to make contact. London said that it was 'someone close to her'. I did not at first think that it might be her brother, for he had disappeared so definitively from the scene that I wasn't prepared for his reappearance as a commando who might be dropped from the air in the LaSalle region, in order to organise Resistance groups which might later make an allied landing from the air a feasibility. As for me, only my hate for him surged up when I found that it was indeed he. Hate! Pure hate!

"It is not the most desirable or elegant of sentiments. I was surprised myself at its force, for I operated in a sort of blind dream-like automatism which seemed to absolve me of any direct moral responsibility. None of what actually came about was circumstantially planned in detail – or at least not by me. Circumstances fell out as they did, as if willed by destiny or fate or whatever. For example, even after I knew that it was Hilary and that he was going to be dropped in the hope of contacting his sister I did not say anything to Liv, though it would have been wise to see what her reaction might be. Would she, for example, have been capable of refusing these overtures on behalf of her brother – indeed, her lover? And then, what did Hilary really hope to gain in making contact? It was hard to see what London was really expecting of the operation. But for my part I was quite filled with exultation to think that I might lay my hands so easily upon the author of all my misfortunes, and that it was in my power to have him done away with the utmost ease, simply by betraying him to the Milice or having the Army arrest him and sentence him. But first we must secure his person. I selected a landing ground with the greatest care, high up in the forests of the Cévennes, and again there was something dreamlike about the ease with which the whole operation took place. He himself was not suspecting anything untoward, and he had received a message through me that his sister would make herself available for a talk. Of course we did not recognise each other after such a long lapse of time – indeed, there really was no reason why we should. We had perhaps seen each other once or twice but we had never actually met in the conventional sense. Indeed I would not now have been quite certain of his identity had I not known from London who it was. It was pitifully simple, his capture and transfer to a jeep to take him to Avignon, and of course by now he knew that he was a prisoner of war, that the plot had failed. I had involved both the Army and the French Milice in the operation so that in a sense he was everybody's prisoner, and this was the start of my troubles because I progressively lost control over him myself – he was locked up for interrogation in the fortress of Avignon where a number of agencies started to interest themselves in his identity and his fate. The fact that he had lived in Provence before the war and knew the place and the language was intriguing for the Milice and they started claiming him as a common-law prisoner – he had not been in uniform when captured. Of course either way it could spell death – both agencies could invoke a firing squad once they had finished their interrogation . . . which was all I really cared about. Unhappily with this turn of events Liv came into view.

"Of course you know that there had always been something equivocal about Livia's life and the way she chose to live it, and there were people who found everything about her somewhat suspect, including her political and philosophic views. In time of war, too, it is the fashion of intelligence agencies to suspect everyone of possible treachery. So that not everyone was friendly to Liv. And the more people knew about her past, and about the family relationship with pre-war Provence, the more intriguing they found her. And now her brother had flown in direct from England with the professed intention of locating her. Well, all these brainless but suspicious creatures who collect around intelligence agencies like a sort of intestinal flora – they began to ask questions, and so indeed did I. The trouble of course was that whatever

they found incriminated Livia, a development for which I had
not really been prepared. When I told her about the arrival
and capture of her brother she went as white as a sheet and
sat down, almost fell down, into a chair, possessed by a total
amazement. And then of course came the realisation that a
sentence of death would be practically a certainty for him.
Can we do nothing to save him, she asked me ironically
enough, and I did not know what to say in reply, for it was
far from my intention to save him. But her emotion was so
intense that I hesitated, while she now said that she must see
him, she must have an interview with him. He had already
been tortured by the unimaginative Milice interrogator and
plied with a great number of routine questions worthy of a
fifth-rate medieval inquisitor, to none of which did he give
anything but evasive answers. It was not a very rich dossier as
intelligence went. But I now persuaded them that there might
be richer material to be found if one organised an interview
between brother and sister of which a recording could be
made if we placed microphones in the place of rendezvous.
They found this reasonable enough, and as a matter of fact
the spot I chose for the encounter was right here in this pew,
where we are sitting! Yes, I know, it is rather queer to choose
the same place again, but I somehow felt it appropriate to our
story – or at least to mine, for I often come here and sit here
alone in order to think about her. I regret so much – and yet
our misfortunes do not seem to be the outcome of our acts
but just due to fate, to destiny! The meetings duly came
about, right here where we are sitting, and the whole thing
was duly recorded by a powerful microphone which I had
installed carefully to transcribe it all on to wax rolls, to which
you may listen if you are so minded. There is hardly anything
about espionage on them – it is all about their extraordinary,
unholy love. It makes my blood curdle as well, for it explained
why our own love miscarried . . ."

He had by now turned quite pale and strained and his recital had a tendency to flag as his story neared its crisis. He came and slumped down beside her in the pew and let his head fall into his hands. He closed his eyes and went on in a lower key. "Of course you may not want to hear it, it may seem too painful. But I was hoping to win your sympathy and confidence by offering the text to you; and, by the way, there is one passage which refers to you in it. It is where Livia says to him: 'You only settled for me because Constance was not available – she was in love with Aubrey: but it was she you really loved, really wanted!' Inextricable the strands of motive which make up the repertoire of a single human heart." (This was Constance's thought, and also: one can become morally responsible for things, situations, desires, of which one is ignorant.)

"Go on," she said in her dry tone of utter amazement, for the whole of this recital had shaken her to the depths. If asked to invent an answer to her questionings she would not have been able to devise anything as baroque as the truth. Hilary and Livia! And then, to cap it, the image of herself as figuring in this history, as accumulating Dharmic guilt for situations she was not even aware of . . . He had started talking again in his halting fashion: "Do you want to hear more, then? It is not a very happy story. Hilary had now become the prisoner not of the Gestapo but of the French Milice whose newly appointed head was a fervently anti-British ex-policeman, avid for advancement. For him even a death sentence hardly satisfied his bloodthirstiness. It hardly satisfied his hate which was nourished on sentiments of secret shame and cowardliness. People who are cowardly enough to cut off women's hair are toneless souls and would cut off anything. That is why we Germans loathed the French so. This bleak and dreadful little man proposed to use the brand-new guillotine which Vichy had sent him to make an example of

Hilary! I wanted this, of course, but I had not worked out in detail just how I would like it; nor had I taken Livia into consideration! I tried to delay the judgement but there was a limit to what I could do, and besides I had lost control of my prisoner now – the French tried and condemned him to death. Meanwhile Livia herself had been picked up and imprisoned for further questioning. The French had been quite intrigued by parts of the interview which seemed to them to promise useful information – rubbish, of course! But meanwhile Livia found herself in the fortress in the next cell to her brother. From the priest who was sent to console them she now learned that Hilary was due to be guillotined on the morning of the next day but one. There was no hope for him as he had been judged by secret tribunal – at that time the police was a law unto itself, and many a private grudge was paid off in this way. There was worse to follow, for in order to punish her also for her resentful and non-cooperative attitude under questioning, it was decreed that she should be forced to witness Hilary's execution in the prison yard where this dreadful toy had been set up at last. The other day I found the day-book of the Milice with the most detailed instructions about the uses of the instrument. Vichy's special tribunals of 14 August 1941 had a military figure as a president and special laws – death sentences for all proven Communists and Anarchists. The first to die was the town tart, a gipsy called Guitte. I remember a few laconic phrases from this record: *M. Défaut, l'exécuteur des hautes oeuvres, a commencé son travail à l'aube, à echancrer la chemise autour du cou, entraver les pieds avec une ficelle et d'attacher les mains derrière le dos* . . . all in great detail. Hilary is there listed simply as *espion anglais*. The guillotine is referred to as *les bois de justice*, or as stags' antlers. Beside it were placed *deux grands corbeilles en osier* by the executioner whose assistant pinioned Livia's arms and dragged her to the site. He was called Voreppe and later he committed suicide because, his wife said, he could not stand the *bruit sourd* of the falling blade which he always seemed to hear in his memory. Hilary struggled and choked, and so did she; there was quite a fight before they managed to force his head into the half moon of steel and release the heavy blade. It was now that she inflicted the wound which cost her her sight, plucking a dirk from the belt of one of the guards. She intended to do away with herself but was forcibly prevented and carried back to the garrison infirmary where she was drugged and put back to bed. It was over!"

He gave a gross sob and fell silent; and so was Constance now, silent for what seemed an eternity during which in her imagination she relived this awful scene, ran it through repeatedly like a cinema film until she felt sick and apprehensive for her reason almost . . . But what could she say? It was she who had sought for answers to certain questions – and here they were, totally unexpected answers! Moreover answers which apparently cost him great pain to formulate and express. She looked at him with curiosity, wondering what the motivation might be of such a performance. Then she said, "What are you expecting of me? I am curious to know."

He sighed profoundly and for a moment seemed at a loss for words. They stared at each other – there were still tears in his eyes as well as hers. "I want," he said, "to meet Lord Galen if possible. I have something important to say to him – something which may make me useful, nay indispensable to him. I know that you know him and that he is somewhere in the region at this moment. Isn't that so?" She watched him with some curiosity as he wound and unwound his fingers, for his pallor was quitting him and this new departure brought a flush to his cheek. "Yes, but why exactly?" she said out of pure perverseness. "I feel you must tell me a good deal more before I trouble old Galen on your behalf!" He made an impatient gesture with his head and said, "Very well, then

I see I shall have to tell you the whole story. I was afraid of boring you, for it does not concern you in any way. But it could concern him, and I might secure his good offices in the question of my trial for enemy activities – it is coming up in Avignon in some months, and I need sponsors of his calibre. It would not be at all compromising for him to intervene and help me because after all I have quite a solid case in my own favour. After all, I *did* work for the British as they will certainly testify. But just to make the whole thing 100 per cent secure I would like to offer Lord Galen something unique, something that he has been looking for for years – the Templar treasure! To go back a little way in history, one of the most helpful collaborators was Dr Jourdain – it's from him that I know all that I do about you all. And at some period in the war he had to hospitalise and sedate a young French clerk called Quatrefrages who had been working for the Galen consortium on the whole Templar problem. It was from him – often it was from his ravings because sometimes he wasn't all there – that I found out how much work and thought had already gone into the project upon which he hoped to found a whole fortune – I suppose a second or third! Of course this interested me very much. When Quatrefages was discharged I kept in touch with him, and by mildly threatening him with the displeasure of the Gestapo I obtained all the historical and topographical material he had accumulated on behalf of Lord Galen and the Egyptian prince who shares this interest. In the meantime a new and different line of inquiry developed from the discovery that the Roman workings of the abandoned mines near the Pont du Gard could be transformed into ammunition caches for all the stuff which was pouring down upon us in the Rhône valley and which we must stack up in some safe place against the day when the big battles for the south of France became a reality, as the German Command thought – and with good reason! But the sappers in charge of the operation were Austrians with a bad record for mutinies and desertions and they went about their work with sabotage in mind. So it was that as fast as they cleaned out the corridors and stacked the incoming ammunition they mined the whole place very thoroughly and in such a way that from a relatively small central explosion they could cause a chain of secondary ones which might blow everything into the air – even the Pont du Gard itself! They wired the whole place up so scrupulously that the five master-keys or detonators could be set in place in a matter of minutes. It was at this time that they stumbled upon the door in the rock which opened into a hollowed-out group of five contiguous caves with cemented walls and stone masonry of high finish. From here they started coming out with precious stones which of course were difficult to sell except to the gipsies, and that is how I got wind of the find, from a gipsy who was 'helping' me with my inquiries into other matters. That is how I got into touch with the sapper Schultz, the drunken sergeant of the troop who together with one other-rank claimed to have made the find and who had locked up the cave, intending to keep this booty for himself. But meanwhile the general situation had deteriorated greatly and we were preparing for a wholesale evacuation. At this point the story of the ammunition train took over. As a parting act of revengeful vindictiveness the General commanding the retreat decided to inflict a mortal blow upon the city. He planted a train full of munitions on the railway bridge and commanded the unit of sappers to boobytrap it as thoroughly as possible so that when the troops had reached a fair distance from the town a skeleton rearguard could set alight to it and cause an explosion of unpredictable violence. Yes, there is no doubt, Avignon would have become a hole in the ground! And at this point the drunkard Schultz who had never performed a coherent act of magnanimity in his whole life, ordered his men to mutiny and refuse! They started to try and barricade themselves into the tunnels but the garrison was ordered out and with a couple of tanks they dislodged them and took the whole lot prisoner. The outcome was not far to seek. They were lined up against the wall in the public cemetery and executed for treachery. Later the townsfolk covered their mass grave with roses to show their gratitude. But while people were found to dig the grave the bodies lay along the wall for nearly a week and I gave myself the disagreeable task of picking them over at night with the aid of lanterns, in search of a map which I knew must exist, a map of the caves with all their secreted ammunition. Otherwise how dare to enter them and search for the treasure? Schultz was the last to die – he was forced to watch all the other executions. The map was on him!

"It took me a little while to work out the code he employed – parts of the glossary are in a kind of electrical shorthand. But I finished by comprehending it, and also the elaborate system of lighting which enables one to light up the whole place; also the grotto which houses the entry and exit system and the keys. There were some obscurities but thanks to what I had learned from my long dialogue with Quatrefages I knew a few things about the quincunx shape of the caves. In architecture the quincunxial shape was considered a sort of housing for the divine power – a battery, if you like, which gathered into itself the divinity as it tried to pour earthward, to earth itself – just like an electrical current does. This magical current was supposed to create an electrical 'field' around the treasure and protect it from being discovered until its emanations were fully mastered and could be used in the alchemical sense to nourish a sort of world bank which might enable man to come to terms with matter – his earthly inheritance, so to speak. It sounds utter rubbish, I know, and I am not personally very much concerned with that aspect of the business. I share Lord Galen's simpler and more practical view of things. I think that riches offer the only tangible safety for a man who has clearly seen how dangerous and horrible his fellow man is. There is no other way of protecting oneself against him except by amassing money and creating a protective power-field of money – that is my view. Well, I wish to try to interest the consortium he represents in my scheme. I am the only living person who can offer safe access to the treasure which otherwise would be out of reach of everyone because of the sheer hazards of the boobytrapping. There is no means at present of evaluating how much is at stake, but the sum must clearly be tremendous, and of course we must keep the secret if we can. I have even gone so far as to secure an official licence to reactivate this abandoned Roman mine with all its workings (fortunately the whole area still belongs to a single family which is delighted to accept a handsome sum for the licence) so that we could place the whole sector out of bounds to the general public while we went to work on the quincunx of little cells . . . You see why I must meet Lord Galen and put this whole matter to him? Of course I shall want equal membership in the consortium, an equal share of the spoils. Goodness me, can't you see the possibilities of such a thing?"

They stared at each other in silence for an eternity. "Yes, I see," she said at last. "I will tell him."

He burst out laughing with delight. So they fell to discussing the details.

FIVE

The Falling Leaves, Inklings

THE GIPSIES KNEW OF THE TEMPLAR TREASURE, EVEN to its location! The knowledge came from Egypt – landscapes of cork oaks ravaged by yellow ants. Honeysuckle grown clear into trees as if it had had a mad desire to perfume the sky. Desert cobras conferring kinghood, smiles like a breath over embers. Tawny dunes, rock doves, hoopoes. The Bedouin shared their love of gold ornaments, the spoil of rifled tombs, sold to the Templars! Lapis lazuli, amethyst, alabaster, tiger's eye, turquoise from the workings in Sinai, mummia!

Notes scattered to the winds of old Provence. Reality is what is completely contemporaneous to itself: we are not completely in it while we still breathe but we yearn to be – hence poetry!

Sutcliffe *loquitur*. A little tipsy? Yes.

Good writing should pullulate with ambiguities.

Whose dead body buzzing with flies?
The dimensions are four but the aggregates five;
Open-ended reality coming alive!

Questions concerning the individual's rights in the matter of buried treasure occupied the waking thoughts of Lord Galen for many weeks, months, now! He found the ideal man to cope with this ticklish matter – a dark, hook-nosed man – nostrils flared: a lawyer who smells the perfume of litigation. He was a Jew from tragic Avignon who had somehow escaped the searches. A Jew is only a Brahmin with a foreskin. Snip. Snip. Snip.

> In age of clones and quarks
> Bless our radioactive larks
> Quinx in her religious quest
> Will one day tower up o'er the rest
> A star-y-pointed pyramid
> To point to where the Grail lies hid
> Within the poet's begging bowl
> Last metaphor for the human soul!

Once poems were nuggets of inner time but we have become experts in not listening – experts in not growing up.

Sitting on his balcony in the Camargue Blanford thought: "The past has just finished becoming the present and here I am. I am still here un-dead. But the desert has covered the breathing and the night has covered the best. Everything (look around you) is as natural as it can be. All nature consents to the code of five. (Five wives of Gampopa, five ascetics in the Deer Park, five skandas.)"

Proust, so attentive to history as Time, as chronology, as reminiscence, never seems to ask at what point the limpid noise of the water-clock or the gravity of the sun-dial's long nose was replaced by clock-time marked by a machine; surely this must have registered the birth of a new type of consciousness? His immortal tick has become our tock.

Blanford sealed up in a poem like a virgin's womb.
"Subsiding from zenith like an old sand-castle,
The sea-lick washing me away balcony by balcony,
By keep and drawbridge, tower, bastion, ravelin and ramp,

By mote and sannery, and so back to dune soon
And then forever dune prime, and then sand, sand, sand,
The endless and uncountable sand."

"Eh, Sutcliffe?
"Can't you understand?

"I am blind sometimes, like old Tiresias,
My eyes are housed in my breasts
This interloping insight is all I have, outwardly
But inwardly whole new kingdoms are there,
Whole new kings and queens unborn,
But alas my eyeballs were scorched out by sea and sand.
Salt-burned, turned inwards upon the Shades,
While someone I may not name or love
Leads me about like a dog."

Her heart and mine have begun a whole dialogue of
sensation; is it possible after such a long time she is going to
acquiesce and love me? Our hearts are like kites with entangled
strings. (Blanford on Constance.)

Miss Bliss who taught him the piano long ago had a very
classy Kensington accent which when she had a head cold
transformed things – singing "The Berry Berry Bonth of
Bay", for example, or reading from *The Furry Tails of Grimm*
or *The Arabian Nates*. The Prince revered her memory. He
often thought of her and smiled puckishly. Lord Galen told
him about one of his business partners. "Someone told him
he looked Jewish when he was asleep, so with great astuteness
he stayed awake all through the occupation!"

Capstone of the sky, blue Vega the darkness
Like an unharnessed cat – blue star,
The vane and lode of sailors once was fixed,

Who now aim at Polaris, their masts
Vast in erection, riding the simple sea.

"Aubrey, you will soon be beginning your novel. At
last! And I shall be leaving you after all this time together,
body and soul plus soul and body. It's been great knowing
you, and I hope the book works as a metaphor for the human
condition, though that sounds pretentious. Only remember
that those two seducers the striking metaphor and the apt
adjective can turn out to be the poet's worst enemies if they
are not held in check."

Tiresias, the old man wearing tits for eyes,
Deep in his vegetative slumber lies.

Her voice lives on in memory
A bruised gong spoke for Livia
Lessivé par son sperme was she.

In the Hotel Roncery the slip hatch
Into Grévin with its wax models
Showing more pure discernment than intelligence.

Sutcliffe took the Prince on a binge or
Spree – a pig in clover he rolled about in
A garden of untrussed trulls.

A sex in her sex like an alabaster dumpling!
Her knickers smelt of gun-cotton, a
Moth-bag of a woman shedding rice-paper,
Powder, cigarette ash and paper handkerchiefs
Which she had twitched once about her lips.
A characteristic groan as he paid in coin.

You'd have been surprised by the tone
He took, the young Catullus with Julius Caesar;
A Tory untrussing a parvenu, dressing down
A political bounder, a tyke. Then later,
A heart shedding its petals, Latin verse.

Sutcliffe's poetry hardly varies ever:

"Come pretty firework untruss
And let me grope thy overplus,
Between the horns of either-or
Be my dilemma, purple whore,
If spring be through, the season's pulse,
Let's teach each other to emulse."

The ego (Affad used to say) is only a sort of negative
for the superlative esoteric state – tiny glimpses of wholeness;
as if light passed through them, printing out a different reality.
He also said: "Love won't live on charity, its demands are
absolute. If she won't love you then your ship is down by the
hull. Aubrey overheard asking S: "What can I do to make you
seem more real?"

Birds do it like young Lesbians do
As lip to lip they tup their tails
In an adhesive swift caress,
The oviposter's carnal hue,
A member short I must confess
They cause each other sweet distress.
But arms thrust to the elbow up
Is how the modern hardies tup!

Mud . . . Merde . . . Mutt . . . love-bewitched in old
Bombay – my think is spunk when thunk . . . chunks of

thought thunk spill spunk. Blanford to Sutcliffe: "Reading your verse is like dragging a pond without ever finding the body."

Tomboy with a clitoris like an ice-skate seeks rational employ. Sutcliffe: "To oblige her I had to bark like her Pekinese long-dead, run over, buried at the bottom of the garden. Until I was hoarse, my dear fellow! Gustav was the name of the Peke."

Paraplegic frolics, geriatric revels! Once upon a time Truth Absolute dwelt with the Sublime and poets knew where they were or thought they did. Now?! And if you can't get your breath because of your asthma how will you cool your nymph's porridge? Man is so weak that he needs the protection of a woman's desire.

> I married a fair maid
> And she was compos mantis,
> We bought a third return
> On a voyage to Atlantis.

> "Happy New Year!" the roysters cried
> While clowning clones their cuddles plied.
> Gaunt Lesbians like undusted harps
> Hung up their woofs and coiled their warps.
> Woof to warp and warp to whoof
> They like their whisky over proof.

> And so one day we
> Reached Atlantis,
> Outside all peacock
> But inside mantis
> Ecco puella corybantis
> Primavera in split panties!

The new day is dawning – women have become sex

service stations: no more attachments, just distributors of friendly faceless lust. Modern girls whose body-image is smashed by neglect. Neither caressed enough nor suckled without disgust nor respected and treated with the awe they deserve. Pious loveless lives . . . Anorexia nervosa the name of tomorrow's nun – spite long ripened in a sense of inadequacy. Insolent lurching looks when flushed and a bit drunk. Man is noble, man is marvellous: he can be monogamous for whole moments at a time!

Poor Blanford with his eternal note-making and notetaking. "Proust, the last great art metaphor in European history, is relative and contingent in its view of life; ego, sensation, history . . . The sign manual is memory, the central notion is that being is advanced through memory – through what is kept artificially alive. History! But history is simply gossip from an eastern point of view – the five senses, the five arts, are its plumage. For after relativity and the field-theory bleakness sets in and the universe becomes cosmically pointless. Relativity does not bring relatedness! *Monsieur est ravagé par le bonheur!* As Flaubert remarks somewhere: "*Moi, je m'emmerde dans la perfection!*"

The fool waits for perfect weather but the wise man grabs at every scrap of wind, every lull. When he was young he headed for Paris, capital of synthetic loves. Tall beauties like well-trained rocking-horses. Love was a jubilant relation, placental in rhythm; we danced the foetal swirl, the omni-amni blues. A thirst for goodness becomes unhealthy. Let yourself embark on the music's great white pinions into Time!

The worldly life is the enemy of the poetic science! Alchemy will out! But holy structures when they go mad plunge into infamy!

The vatic mule, our German Poet, where was he when the killing was rife? The language is so glutinous that it is like investigating the nervous system of a globe artichoke.

The post-war world has started to form itself in Provence. In the village, Tubain, they have started drinking *pastis* with the old tumefied air, and playing at *boules*. It is reassuring. Even the human type has come back – the true Mediterranean loafer – sleep eats into him like an antacid into a dissenting Anabaptist! A purse under each eye and one under his waistcoat which stirs when he breathes as if a mole were trying to surface. A huge brown nose like Cromwell, full of snot. A Protestant mind packed tight as Luther's big intestine with golden turds – alchemical fruit. The minority dream is to make the parochial universal – the whole universe a suburb with an *accent faubourgienne*! Whiffs of red wine and underclothes – the love calls of a mouthful of dripping crumpet. An analysis of figments! Here, honey, chew on this crust, death!

Problem of woman – lightning never strikes twice in the same place. That heavenly gloating walk, as sultry as Achilles upon a bed of glowing embers!

Today Sutcliffe was washing his hair and singing tunelessly – his theme was "What shall we do with a drunken sailor?" to which he had harnessed words of his own devising, namely, "What shall we do with our alter ego?" I suppose when the time comes you will force me to commit *suttee* – climb on to a pyre and disappear in a swirl of smoke and a delicious odour of frying bacon. My apotheosis will have begun – myself transformed into the Swami Utter Conundrum with his three free-wheeling geishas, preaching the way to Inner Umptiousness. Swami so full of inner magnetism that he sparks as he describes the new reality: "If you can leave it alone sufficiently you will discover that reality is bliss – nothing less! When the mathematical and the poetical co-exist as they were always meant to; a collision of worlds takes place and you write a hymn to Process. It's love that beckons, that huge axiomatic doll that we kiss to three places of decimals. In her arms you realise that happiness is just despair turned inside out like a sleeve. You ask yourself, "What am I as an artist but a whimsical poacher of stallion's eggs?"

To investigate what went wrong with the intellect of a civilisation one has to start with human perception . . . i.e. sex, the original form of knowing which preceded language . . . i.e. telling, formulating, realising!

> sweet thumbs up
> dark thumbs down
> life's for living
> says the clown
> nothing adventured
> nothing said
> slip off to join
> the laughing dead!

Smirgel took every kind of precaution against declaring where he was living or how, and for a while all trace of him was lost – so much so that the Prince began to wonder whether the whole rigmarole of his story was not invented, perhaps for obscure motives. Then the air cleared and he telephoned to Constance and offered them a rendezvous at the little bistro on the road to Vers which had recently changed hands and reopened. Sunlight greeted them under the olives. He was already there when they arrived in the Prince's great Daimler which had once belonged to Queen Mary! In the sparkling shadow and light of the glade with its green tables Smirgel looked what perhaps he really was at heart, a wandering German professor of history on holiday. But he rose to greet them and his ankles sketched the faintest shadow of a Prussian heel-click – out of respect for the two dignitaries who came forward to meet him full of a delicious sense of legitimate cupidity – the folklore of riches! The Prince's natural affability was very fetching, he exuded warmth. They all sat down and eyed each other for a long moment of silence, until a waiter came out of the bar and procured them drinks of their choice. Smirgel was nervous and ordered water.

After a silence during which the Prince politely toasted his guests in rather indifferent champagne Smirgel said, "Lord Galen, I feel we can afford to be frank now. I trust my reasons for wanting to meet you have become clear to you. I explained everything about the treasure to Constance and asked her to retail it to you in the hope of gaining your attention because I know that you and your consortium of interested backers are Geneva-based and serious – *des gens sérieux, quoi*! I am quite confident that what I have to offer them is of interest even though for the moment I cannot evaluate how much is actually at stake. The point is that nobody alive has access to it because of the pure danger inherent in the situation – the explosives and the mining! But what I can offer them is a detailed map of the boobytrapping with which one can gain safe access in order to visit and assess it. I have seen some of the precious stones and have spoken to the man who discovered it, so I know that it is not a fantasy but a fact. In exchange I would naturally wish to be represented among the other speculators, and entitled to my legitimate share of the booty."

"I must admit that the thought of an immense fortune makes me sentimental," said Lord Galen dreamily, but the Prince sounded a trifle reproachful when he said, "Yes, but think of the pure historical beauty of the thing – to rediscover this long-lost and far-famed treasure! We mustn't lose sight of the cultural aspect, for many of the articles must be things of great beauty and we must keep a careful record for the future of our find." The German sat quietly smoking and watching them with attention. The Prince's mind roved far and wide among the legends and folktales of his own land, Egypt where secret treasures buried in caves and guarded by malefic djinns were a commonplace. "It would be amusing," he said, "if the treasure had been filched away and had been replaced with feathers or sand!" He chuckled, but neither Galen nor the German found this line of thought funny. "How soon can we be sure?"

The German smiled and replied, "Just as soon as I am prepared to release to you the map of the workings. Then we can just walk into the caves and locate the door and force it. Presto! But this I will not do until the articles of association are signed and I am happy in my mind about my part."

"A limited company, based on Geneva, called Treasure Trove Incorporated," said Galen dreamily. "But how shall we describe the site? I have all the means to create the document."

The German pulled forth from under him – he had been seated on it – a battered briefcase which contained two documents of importance: a cadastral map of the workings with scales and numbers and the names of the owners.

The German continued his exposition in a leisurely style and in the tone of a lecturing professor, but the matter was impeccably organised and the English choice. "I have discovered that practically the whole section which concerns us is in the possession of one single family, and I have already made contact with them. They are peasants and pretty hard up so that they have been delighted to rent the whole section to me on a hundred-year lease; on my side I have been into the legal side of things and have obtained a government lease and a permit to work the land and exploit the resources. French law is coming back into force and civil considerations are coming to the fore. I hinted that what I had in mind was to reactivate the Roman quarry as there were many unexploited seams still bearing, and this would of course provide employment in the area which would be welcomed. Indeed this will have to be our cover-story, so to speak, as we would not wish to excite the French government with tales of buried treasure upon which they might have a tax claim. However, in the present state of things I see no major reason why we should not extract the treasure, bit by bit if necessary, and maintain a cover-front of quarrymen to work the seams in good faith. Do you see anything against it?"

Lord Galen saw nothing against it. "But the famous map of the quarry – where is that?"

"It is in my possession, in a safe place, and at your disposition when certain conditions have been fulfilled. Chief among them is of course my acquittal by the war crimes tribunal which have put me mistakenly on their black list. In two months' time my case comes before them, by which time I hope that Lord Galen will have acted for the defence and pulled the scales down in my favour. This whole business is due to the vanity and jealousy of the Milice. They would like to get me branded or beheaded or imprisoned because of all I know about their behaviour during the bad years. They have much to hide, as you may well suppose. But I think it will be possible to get a fair verdict in my favour especially because of the British members of the ruling committee. I am sure Lord Galen knows them all and can put in a word for me. I have their names on this piece of paper." He passed over the documents in question and Lord Galen saw with horror that there were several friends on the list, while the president of the tribunal was one of his shareholders! He swallowed and blinked. "As soon as I am acquitted you will have the map.

But in the meantime let us work out the articles of association and get everything ready for action."

He conducted them across the quarry to where the entrance was, picked out by the tall entrances to the caves, some quite profound. "We are concerned", he said, "with the sequence of caves which begins here, on the left-hand side. I have managed to get the family which owns the land to close off the entrance as far as is possible in order to avoid trespassers of any sort. I have had several scares concerning the place. On one occasion a shepherd used them to shelter his flock during a thunderstorm: drove a hundred sheep into the entrance. My blood ran cold – I happened to be across the way, sheltering myself in a cave-entrance. It was too late to stop the shepherd, for he had followed his sheep into the first corridor. When I told him the danger he faced he went as white as a sheet and started to whistle up his dogs to retrieve the sheep, which by this time had scattered into the various corridors. Psychologically we both kept our fingers in our ears and hardly dared to breathe for what seemed eternity, until the last sheep had been retrieved and chased back into no man's land. What an escape! One sheep could easily have fouled a trip wire and set off the whole place by a mass explosion. But of course once we start work seriously we must enforce strict security measures until we have cleared the place – or as much of it as is necessary for the work we have in mind."

(Blanford had noted in his Ulysses archive: when the Cyclops cries, "Who goes there?" and Ulysses nervously replies "Nobody", it constitutes the first Zen statement in the European literary canon!)

Walking back across the olive-glades they reached a working agreement as to the procedure to be invoked in order to harness all their interests together. Smirgel gave them a phone number where they might contact him if need be and then took his leave astride an ancient push-bike, melting slowly into the landscape with slow strokes of the pedals. "Well I never," said the Prince, summoning another drink in order to talk over the whole matter with his partner. "If this comes off it will be something quite unique, no?"

"Indeed!" said Galen with a sort of uncertain rapture. The Prince added, "Are you going to use your pull and try to get him off?" Lord Galen nodded vehemently. "He won't be any use to us if he's sent up for life and won't tell where the map is, will he? He must be kept cooperative, don't you think? The whole thing is far from settled, I think. But it's promising, I agree, dashed promising, and we must pursue it single-mindedly." He put on his single-minded look and gazed round him like a blind buzzard. He had borrowed the look from a bust of Napoleon on St Helena which stood on his desk at home.

SIX

The Return

WHEN SHE SAW HIM STANDING THERE IN THE HALL of Tu Duc beside his luggage, leaning on a stick and clad in his old much-darned Scotch plaid, she could not resist a wave of tenderness, so much did his presence evoke of their common youth – a whole summer passed here in these enchanted glades and meadows in that limbo before The Flood! He too was overtaken by an involuntary shyness and hesitation. "Are you sure you want me here, fouling up your life with my heavy sighs?" But they embraced tenderly enough and she put on her briskest medical tone in order to hide her emotion. "I really wanted you under my eye, in my hands, because I noticed that you are slacking off on the yoga and simply not getting the massage you need for your back. At least that I can guarantee myself, while of course here you can swim in the mill-stream every day which is a radical part of the treatment. I propose to take you in hand."

He could not imagine anything more delightful to contemplate and he settled into Livia's room with its old Freudian couch without very much ado; his few clothes and books and his clutch of notebooks found niches easily enough, and once his possessions were in order he descended with his queer swaying walk to the kitchen where he proposed to help her cook the lunch – she was expecting the Prince and Lord Galen after their interview with Smirgel. They were both good cooks by now, and this was a further bond which was ripening between them. Somehow a profound reserve reigned in a strange sort of way, for there were a hundred questions he was dying to put to her though the time and place had not yet somehow come into focus – it was not yet appropriate to do so. And of course when their guests arrived the redoubled activity absorbed them and provided a neutral background against which all conversation became not personal but general. The Prince for example had been highly exhilarated by his encounter with the German but was as yet not fully convinced of his *bona fides*. He plied Constance with questions about him. Galen on the other hand had swallowed the whole proposition wholesale. "What other thing could he have been thinking?" he asked plaintively, and, "One has to learn to trust *someone* or one never gets results. I think the story is true, and if we play our cards right we will win out!"

On this genial note the lunch party embarked on the dishes that Constance had prepared. "I shall see to it that your name is on the list of shareholders," the Prince told her, "if only because of the excellence of this *boeuf gardien*."

The Prince had spent the previous afternoon visiting the half-yearly fair of the city, some aspects of which had filled him with misgivings, such as the bold red inscriptions on the walls of the churchyard talking of alien matters. The first American tourists had arrived in Avignon!

> Skinheads Rule!
> Yes! Yes!
> Madness Reigns!
> Yes!
> Kill everyone!
> Yes! Yes!

It was the new world they had hatched beginning to stake out its claims on the future. The Prince permitted himself a premonitory shudder or two and allowed a chill to trickle down his spinal column as he visualised this hallowed countryside being invaded by representatives of the American industrial ethos. Nearer home, too, and hardly less disturbing was a British representative of Tyneside who at least had some redeeming touches of Golgotha humour to salt his act. This was a young man, Suckathumbo Smith by name, who sat in front of a curtain on which was depicted a scene from circus life – a dentist in frock coat extracting a tooth against the will of a young woman in a crinoline. Smith was a chunky young man and his eyes had been completely circled in mascara like the spectacles on the hood of a cobra. He looked tear-stained, as if he had cried all night, and when not using his voice kept himself corked up so to speak, thumb in mouth. He would suddenly remove the thumb and let forth a shriek of song, and then as suddenly plunge his thumb back into the aperture, sinking as he did so into a posture of despair and gloom. Blanford delighted in him as a curiosity, and would not leave his booth until the whole performance was at an end. The last act was a spirited rendering of the old Cockney classic:

> Uncle Fred and Auntie Mabel
> Fainted at the breakfast table
> They forgot the gipsy's warning
> Not to do it in the morning!

This at least had the hallmarks of true music hall on it and was as true to its tradition as Shakespeare would have been. But such manifestations made uncomfortable bedfellows for the folklore subsidised by tourist organisations in the hope of making foreign visitors feel at home. And indeed the first foreign visitors had hardly begun to show their faces as yet. The post-war city was a sort of limbo for the moment, quite uncertain of its possibilities, urged on only by the prestige of its past.

But spring was at hand, the sunny days not too far off, and this gave them the opportunity to transfer their morning therapies of massage and yoga to a more suitable spot, namely the flat rocks around the weir with its grave menhirs and abandoned threshing floor. Here the river swept by in a sudden convulsion of pleasure among the water lilies. Here one could lie and drowse or read, lulled by the water-music of the Roman weir. Constance was very businesslike about the work and Blanford grumbled but obeyed her, allowing the doctor full rights over her patient, though the feel of her capable brown hands settling on his back and beginning to manipulate the muscle schemes thrilled him sexually until he felt shy to feel the incipient half-erection which the therapy caused him, and wondered if she was aware of the fact. She was, and the thought gave her a twinge of irritated self-reproach. But it would pass – so she opined – familiarity would breed contempt! She need only persevere. And talk about other things. "I must say, Aubrey, they have done you a superb job of renovation." He grunted his assent and added: "All done up like an expensive tennis racquet with the best gut and steel wires. I am unbelievably lucky. And now to continue the massage with you . . ." Part of it, too, was the swimming. They took off side by side and paddled slowly up river among the lilies, talking, or else in a companionable silence betimes. A new kind of intimacy was hatching itself between them which, for the moment, they could not identify or classify. She spoke to him now quite wordlessly, while she was working on his back. "How strange that you should be my first love, my worst love," she told him. "The only one with whom I could make no progress whatsoever. And of course I yours – I would have been an idiot not to recognise the fact. What went wrong? I found you frigid, autistic and quite self-obsessed – but now, looking back on it, I wonder whether it wasn't simply timidity? Those English schools drive one back into oneself and remove all spirit of enterprise where girls are concerned." Blanford had fallen asleep like a cat under the effect of the massage. She frowned, for it was obvious that his psyche was reacting to the massage as if to caresses – and this was not what the doctor in her approved or had in mind.

"Aubrey! Wake up!" she said, "And let's go for a swim up to the point. The sun is westering." He grumbled but complied. "I dreamed we made love," he said grimly, "and that at last it worked between us. You were after all my first love." She frowned and acquiesced reluctantly. "And I yours?" After a pause, "Yes. Very much so!"

There was a long silence.

Then he said, "Christ! What on earth went wrong, do you think? And is it redeemable?" She laughed and spread out her arms in a rueful gesture. "Of course not!" she said, but gaily, "look at us both, so battered from the wars and the whole blessed attrition of time passing . . . We've overshot the mark!" It was depressing, nay, intolerable to believe that she might be right. It made him suddenly realise how permanent the image of her had been – even when she herself was not present, even when he had not been conscious of the fact, she had been overwhelmingly present in his mind, his heart. "You have always been so very much part of the décor; I don't think I have made any decisions or thought any thoughts without mentally referring to you – I mean, even when you were with Affad you were still a sort of lodestar to me! It's queer! In anyone else it would be accounted for by the word 'love'. But I don't dare! I am afraid you would protest!

"I can't flirt any more. But I can still dare, so in a sort of way I am still open to adventure. But so much has changed in my outlook. After he died I realised, but quite slowly, that I could not love again in the old way, in the literary way, as if from a dialectical frenzy. Yet paradoxically the new freedom which came to me from his death freed me to love more truly, more correctly, while at the same time remaining my own master. It was deeper and chaster despite its freedom. Yes, I could not any more enter into the great engagement and surrender myself wholly. I'm on the threshold of middle age, I suppose that is it."

He listened to her with the silence of misgivings, for what is more hopeless than for a woman to try and analyse the nature of love and its thousand forms and dispositions? He said, "I have been watching his wonderful little son to whom you have managed to bring so much that you have really succeeded in being a mother to him. In him I get a wonderful feeling of self-sufficiency, of estrangement from all formal joy. I feel sure he is going to be an artist. He looks about him with the disabused eye of one – the feeling of being able to see through things, to discern their coarse primal roots, their quiddity, and hence their boredom with God! It's only a manner of speaking, but how to convey his marvellous detachment? I was like he is, an autist, a complete virgin, which unluckily you could not possess – to my eternal loss. Had you managed to wake me from my death-sleep I would have blessed you for the rest of my life! But no, it was not to be, I had to sleep my way forward by years in order to catch up with you here, on this rock, after a long and miserable war. How strangely life arranges things!"

Another comic paradox of fate was the drift of Blanford's notes which he had so carefully emptied to the four winds; a large section had blown about the city until the curious gipsy children had started to amass them and show them to their parents. From there to the consultation of a bookseller was but a step, and it was not long before Toby was offered a bundle of scraps for sale, which he had at once recognised from the handwriting as belonging to Blanford who expressed himself prepared to buy them back, presuming that the mere fact that they had escaped destruction was a portent concerning their value for his forthcoming book whose presence had begun to loom up strangely over his future life. Now that he was more or less physically restored to daily life the question of an occupation had begun to nag at him. He was glad that his tiny income did not prevent him from addressing himself to literature as a possible means of making money. It would have been bad for him, he thought, if private means had freed him from the onus of thinking coldly and professionally of the novel as a wage-earner. And then there was another thing – for how long could he support a brother-to-sister relationship with Constance? Their relationship could not forever stay like this, in solution so to speak, without any sort of physical development: or could it? His breasts ached when he thought about her! How stupid people were! He lay softly breathing under the determined thoughtful fingers which prowled his back and shoulders while he riffled the latest bundle of scraps to have emerged from the hands of the gipsies. A novelist forced to buy back his own notes – what a farce!

Is meditation an art or a science? Discuss.
Strawberries are neither classical nor romantic. Discuss!
By simple oxygen and silence slip
Into the Higher Harmlessness!

To this Sutcliffe had added a rider, which went: "But the Hindu is as high-minded as he is long-winded. Heaven preserve us from such a cataplasm, however much he may be right theologically."

He added: "What a curse self-importance is! If we would only shut up and give nature a chance to talk we would certainly learn that Happiness, nay, *Bliss* is innate!"

But circumstances do not always show themselves as cooperative to human designs and they were soon thrown together without equivocation by a simple incident which grew out of their habit of night-swimming. Despite the relative earliness of the season they had enjoyed almost a fortnight of hot weather, real summer weather, and this had pushed them to revert once more to the once popular habit of swimming at night off the stone, using as light the one hissing gas-light of which the house boasted. This they propped on the rock. Its rather ghostly yellow light which flapped and flared outlined a small central circle of water among the lilies sufficient to constitute virtually a round shining pool of water. They tried to keep within its limits in the interests of good order and indeed safety, but it was not always possible, so strong was the tug of the water round the rock. Nevertheless that was the scheme, and they were sufficiently practised and confident, both of them, to embark for a swim even if alone. This is what had happened on the night in question – Constance had gone on ahead; crossing the dark garden with his slow swaying walk he could see the flap and flare of the light standing on the stone plinth above the water. He heard the sound of her plunge and then the noise of paddling and treading water – all perfectly in order. It would be difficult to say just what it was that alerted him to the fact that all was *not* in order; perhaps he overheard her gasp of dismay as she turned on her back – dismay to feel a sudden rogue cramp attack her thighs and legs, a reaction from the cold of the water. But with a current so formidable there was little time to be lost if the situation was to be redressed – and there was no shore to speak of, for the lilies were anchored in three metres of silt. "Are you all right?" he called anxiously, for he had sensed that something had gone wrong. "Yes! No!" she cried in her disarray. It was a double deception, for Aubrey in his present situation was not at the peak of his powers as a swimmer, and it would be unfair to call him into the water . . . Nevertheless her distress conveyed itself to him rapidly enough and he saw that the only thing to do was to throw himself in after her and try to help her master the tugging current which was trying to pull her downstream. In still water there would have been no problem – she could have floated for ever; but the current created a possible hazard. She heard him plunge after her and her heart misgave her – they might both be in trouble because of this rashness. But he was stronger than he himself had quite supposed and seizing her under the arms he turned doggedly back up-current, determined to put them both within finger-reach of the stone plinth, their point of entry into the water. At first, and for a long moment, the issue hung in the balance even though he put forth his utmost endeavour, stroke on slow stroke. Then with infinite slowness he began to gain against the water. It was a matter of a mere two or three metres but the issue was a critical one, for the water was trying its best to sweep them down river to where the Roman ford created a sort of small but vertiginous waterfall. Here the current might be strong enough to create an accident of sorts – a knock on the head, a broken wrist, something of that order. But his slow and concentrated stroke was sufficiently masterful to begin to gain on the current, and at last he had a satisfaction and relief of pushing his fellow swimmer to a point where her fingers could grasp the serrated edges of rock and haul herself clear of the current, but at the same time holding fast to his hand with the other arm. Thus with infinite slowness and infinite labour they at last managed to clear the water and crawl ashore to the safety of the rock – there to tumble in an exhausted heap. "I have never had a cramp before," she said, among her apologies for having dragged him after her, "I had no idea one could just freeze up, like that." And of course concern for his back now seized her – he might have sprained or dragged a muscle by his efforts, and nothing would satisfy her but to see for herself. But here something radical had changed – the whole cloud of inhibitions which had paralysed him in his dealings with her suddenly seemed to have lifted. Was it perhaps the fleeting terror of losing her for ever to the river that had purged him? A classical boldness now beset him, he took her in his arms unerringly, as if he were completely sure of her response. They stood like that, enlaced and in silence for what seemed an eternity. Outside in the tall trees the owls screeched and hunted; the lamp which usually stood beside them on the kitchen table gave forth its buzzing commentary – like the noise at the centre of the chambered nautilus. "How marvellous," he whispered, "not to be afraid any longer of making a mess of you! You gave me such a fright with your cramp that it shocked me back into sense. Fear of losing you for ever! I realise everything now. You have learned the most important thing a woman can learn from a man – not from me but from Affad: the art of surrender which assures everything. How grateful I am to him as well!" Nor was this mere verbiage for it translated itself into caresses later that night which were as generous as they were famished. He could still make love then, still generate the power and the glory of the complete sexual encounter. Where the devil had it all come from? He was at a loss to tell.

And like lovers at any time and everywhere they suddenly found the need for privacy overwhelming; so much so that for several weeks after this critical re-evaluation of their loving they almost went out of circulation as far as their friends were concerned – preferring to dine early and lock up at an early bedtime rather than dawdling over dinner, even by moonlight, which was the time-honoured way of treating the slow Provençal nightfall. He found himself jealous not of her person but of her company. Nor was this change lost upon the Prince whose intuition was Egyptian in its sharpness of focus. "It's happened at last," he said with a chuckle in his most pleased and shocked tone of voice. "I shall be writing to the Princess, and I shall tell her that her worst fears have been confirmed! The spectre of love has begun to hang over this pious old bachelor's head. Eh, Constance?" But she was sunk so deeply into the luxury of this marvellous pristine attachment that she was not put out of countenance by his banter. "She will be delighted," she said, "the Princess has always had a soft corner for Aubrey and rather pitied his isolation." Indeed the Prince was highly delighted and was already writing his letter in his head. As for Lord Galen, he had not noticed anything and he became plaintive when the Prince pointed out the obvious to him. "No one ever tells me anything," he said with a sigh, "but I suppose it is a Good Thing, if you say so."

"I most certainly do," said His Highness with his characteristic tone, trenchant and cocksure. But it was less pleasant when the lovers disappeared from circulation for a few weeks, and rumour had it that they were somewhere secret in Italy. They were much missed by the Prince who was hopelessly gregarious and could not live without a staple diet of courtly gossip. Then, as if to complete the catalogue of unexpected happenings, Constance began to believe that she was pregnant and this provoked a further revision of options, a further period of reflection upon the future. It was mar-vellous to think about, and all the more so because neither had really foreseen such an eventuality, though at no time had any precautions been taken to obviate the fact. Blanford was highly delighted in a tremulous sort of way; he had begun to worry about being inadequate as a father and family man. "Does the man having nothing to do spend his time yawning and riffling a dictionary of Christian names? Surely you can set me to work doing something useful?" But for the moment she took her pleasure in encouraging his shiftlessness and the incoherence of his passion. She realised somewhere deep down that this sort of crisis would either make him or lose him!

To wake and find her arms round him – it surprised him to realise his former loneliness: how had he not been more conscious of the felicity of loving, the thrilling beauty of sharing? It was unnerving to find himself surprised like an adolescent at these departures into fine feeling, tenderness, passion. And then to find himself still thirsty and heartwhole after her love had passed over him, so to speak, parched anew like a landscape after rain. Sutcliffe wore a slightly reproachful air these days, but it was probably a case of sour grapes though he had never claimed to be in love with Constance himself, which would have provided an explanation of the fact. Fragments of rejected notebook material kept turning up, too, to add colour to the growing mountain of *obiter dicta* which one day would be polished and sited in the projected novel. He claimed to have invented the "extra-marital biscuit" as well as crumbless bread, not to mention the dildo called Recompense; it had wings and a snout which developed uterine suction by a system of spontaneous nibble. It was full of camshaft glory. Listen to the music of the spheres – the clash of Hercules' testicles. "Enough!" cried Blanford. "In God's name, enough!"

With the first days of summer weather the newly constituted tribunals set up to judge war crimes began to sit in the city, and the question of Smirgel's guilt or innocence would soon come under debate. The whole subject was still confused and riddled with suppositions and false testimony. A typical search for heroes as well as scapegoats was going forward. Two members of the Judge Advocate's staff were plied with attestations highly favourable to Smirgel, while the Prince found them places on the board of the treasure company and a promise of a share in the spoils. You would have thought from the way he went on that the German had been put up for a British DSO as well as the French Military Cross. It was hardly surprising that the case against him was quashed "for lack of conclusive evidence". Meanwhile the courts had the good grace to publish the figures concerning the missing, which showed very clearly that Provence had taken a terrible beating from the Nazis. Of the 600,000 forced labourers sent into Germany 60,000 did not return, 15,000 were shot or beheaded, while 60,000 contracted tuberculosis . . . But the tribunal's judgement on Smirgel was highly delightful, indeed was music to the ears of Lord Galen, for now nothing could stand in the way of their treasure-hunting. The company too had been set up to exploit their gains when the time came.

But here again unexpected factors came into play, among them the fact that rumours of their find had somehow leaked out – perhaps Smirgel had committed a calculated indiscretion? At any rate the city fathers and the authorities in Avignon made it known that they would expect to be kept informed and that any treasure trove which accrued from their activities should be brought to the notice of the museum authorities and the civic authorities. "Bang goes any hope of keeping it secret, but perhaps we can limit the affair to a couple of bribed officials?" said the Prince, swallowing his disappointment as best he could. "Anyway, let's not get worked up in case there is no treasure, or so little as not to be of interest." Lord Galen put on his wistful-alarmed look. At any rate Smirgel had now only to wait for the official judgement which would restore him to the world as innocent, and he was free to produce his map and lead the expedition into the caves. "I don't think we should be dog-in-the-mangerish about letting the officials come in at least for the initial discovery. It is of course a fact of great historic importance and under French law they might even consider impounding the whole thing in the name of the Louvre. Still, for the moment they have not gone as far as that and I think with a few judicious bribes we can get them to shrug their shoulders and declare the find of little interest – something like that."

The era of enlightened self-interest had dawned, it was obvious, and everyone was going to become a millionaire overnight! Yet there were pockets of misgiving here and there. "Are you really confident in the *bona fides* of your map? I wanted to ask you that before," said Lord Galen, and Smirgel cleared his throat and nodded vigorously. "After all, it is only logic for Schultz to keep a copy which would enable him to come back in peacetime and retrieve the treasure; can you see anything wrong with the reasoning? I can't. He would hardly have held on to a dud map, would he?"

No, it stood to reason the map he had hidden about his person was a valid one. It could not be otherwise! On this optimistic note they separated for a day or so to allow all the papers to be sifted into some sort of provisional order. Details for the treasure hunt would be dealt with very shortly. One of the strokes of luck had been the discovery of Quatrefages – his opinion on the affair would be, everyone felt, invaluable. The doctor had kept in touch with him, and he was proposing to come back and work for the Prince once again; but he had become very old-looking, and his hair was quite white. But he had retrieved a good part of his documentation concerning the Templars and hoped to round off his studies with a long essay about them.

Once or twice, in order one supposes to whet their appetites, Smirgel led them as far as the entrance to the main grotto which had been barred to the public with wooden palisades bearing the word "*Danger*" and the phrase "*Défense d'entrer*". They hung about in a desultory sort of way here, discussing ways and means and rather hoping that the German would decide to unburden himself of the famous map, but he was dogged and obstinate, and waited upon the document of the war crimes tribunal. Meanwhile there was another small flutter of excitement, for Quatrefages had unearthed a gipsy in Avignon who claimed to have wandered into the caves by accident and to have actually seen the treasure. According to him the door which Smirgel had firmly closed had opened again and one could enter the caves – or at any rate he had done so and had seen the massive oak trunks with their heaps of precious stones and various sorts of ornament. From these he had extracted a single ruby which he had had fixed in a

nostril. Later on when he had learned of the danger he had
run he had been horrified – but like everyone else he could
not push the affair any further for lack of a guide or a map
with the necessary instructions. Now, of course . . . But while
his testimony sounded valid enough there was something
about the man which did not inspire confidence – a suggestion
of feverish hysteria which made one wonder whether he had
not been fabulating in order to find out something to his
profit.

A still further complication was the arrival on the scene
of the new Préfet of the country who at once asked if he might
address them all on a topic which concerned him as it affected
law and order in the province. It was not possible to refuse,
and the courteous elderly gentleman duly presented himself
before the board which was holding its first executive meeting
at the Pont du Gard in order to discuss dates and means for
the final act. The Prince, Lord Galen, Smirgel and Quatrefages were the most important executives, while vaguer
associates like, for example, the doctor Jourdain, played
backgammon with Blanford and Sutcliffe in the garden. The
Préfet who, like all Frenchmen, had a strong sense of occasion,
ordered champagne all round, before rising to his feet to toast
the Prince and open the ball with a polished little speech. "I
expect you will wonder why I intruded upon your deliberations. Gentlemen, it is to ask you to have some charitable
thoughts about my own problems. Avignon is a thorny place,
and among other thorns I have always to keep our gipsies in
mind. It is a quite large colony and they provide us with a
number of headaches – worse really than Marseilles. But it
would be ill-advised for a governor not to humour them
because they are not only troublesome but also extremely
useful to him. Practically all police intelligence of any depth
and cogency has been sifted and evaluated by the gipsies
before it reaches us at the executive level. Naturally one of

my first tasks has been to make their acquaintance and find out if there is any way in which I can show myself as prepared to be an obliging and friendly patron to the tribe of Saint Sara – such a little gesture goes down very well as you can imagine! And in the course of these manoeuvres I happened upon a remarkable English woman turned gipsy – a daughter of a certain Lord Banquo who may be familiar to you. She has proved a mine of useful information and penetrating judgements, and it was largely on her advice that I hit upon the notion of visiting your organisation.

"It was from her that I learned that long before the Austrian sappers started their ammunition stockpiling in these caves the gipsies kept a grotto here as a chapel sacred to Saint Sara where baptisms and initiations took place at certain times of the year. Yes, the 'tenebrous one' was a flourishing cult figure – sometimes she even encouraged prophecy and the gift of tongues. Naturally the Germans threw out the gipsies when they started stocking the caves. I have been asked to keep these facts in mind if ever there should be a question of spring-cleaning the place and defusing the ammunition contained in the caves. Obviously your own preoccupations centre upon the same matters though for a different set of reasons. I am hereby asking for the sympathy and the good offices of your board when such matters are undertaken in the near future. You will understand that in my present position I can hardly refuse to return the grottoes to Saint Sara whose old mud statue and icons must still be knocking about inside. So far I have only made one approach – I have sounded out Herr Smirgel, and he is perfectly agreeable to a gipsy representation on the first exploration, who will follow him into the caves just as soon as he gets his clearance from the war crimes tribunals. Ouf!"

He paused, somewhat out of breath after so long a disquisition, and gazed from face to face with a self-confident diffidence – for when had his charm failed to convince? But the Prince betrayed a certain disconsolate dismay. There would be far too many people in the know, he opined, and most specially semi-official agencies like the Beaux Arts with largely undemarcated areas of responsibility. Suppose the treasure proved to be not only tangible but immense . . . The whole thing was becoming too swollen for his liking, it was sliding out of control, for now they were even talking of making a photographic record of the findings – to film each item as it was disinterred!

"O dear!" said Lord Galen who had been listening with an expression of ruefulness, for he had begun to enumerate in his mind the number of things which could or might go wrong and qualify their own hold upon the treasure. (And yet suppose there is no bloody treasure, he kept thinking!)

As for Smirgel, he had chosen his day after due and weighty consultations with Quatrefages, aware that it would have to satisfy certain mystical provisions. It must, for example, be a Friday Thirteen in order to echo not only the Name Day of Sara in her prophetic form but also to echo the fatal day when the Order of Templars was abolished. Why does one instinctively seek a continuity in things as if synchronicity satisfied some deep cosmic need? (The question was posed by Blanford to himself and answered with: "Because you fool the world of consciousness is a world of historic echoes which cry out to be satisfied. One grabs at every connection. For example the Templars were abolished in that dismal town Vienne where I once spent ten days in winter haunted by a simple historic fact which I had picked up somewhere – namely, that Pontius Pilate when he retired from the civil service chose Vienne as his town of residence because he found Rome too noisy and too sophisticated and too expensive for a poor pensioner of the state." The result of that visit was a little monograph purporting to be his memoirs written here. It was called "The Memoirs of PP" and it received a condescending but friendly review by Pursewarden.)

"For months afterwards," added Sutcliffe, "I dreamed all night of washing my hands in a silver ewer to the baying of a scruffy crowd of subhumans!"

At teatime the old Daimler of the Prince hove in sight with Cade at the wheel; he had come from the Tubain post office with a cargo of mail from the central sorting agency in Avignon which had only half-resumed its civil functions. With these heterogenous letters there was one familiar buff envelope superscribed OHMS and addressed to Smirgel. He had not given the Judge Advocate General his true address but that of Lord Galen since they were friends. It was the magical certificate for which he had been so anxiously waiting. It attested to his innocence of any war crime. He gave a sob as he unfolded the document. Then he tenderly embraced Cade, kissing him on both cheeks. Then he held up the paper and cried, "Look, everybody, this is the certificate of clearance – I am declared innocent, and can resume civil life again as an ordinary citizen of the world! Ah! you can't know what it means! But as for the treasure we can go ahead now and plan the event in all seriousness." To their surprise he fell on his knees and said a prayer.

SEVEN

Whether or Not

BLAN: "ADMIT YOU WERE JEALOUS: YOU DID NOT LIKE to see me slipping out of your grasp, did you?"

SUT: "I admit it. I felt insulted that you would not tell me the truth. I knew full well that you were not in Siena or Venice or Athens . . ."

BLAN: "No. We were hidden in the Camargue in a little cottage lent to us by Sabine. After this strange episode, the kisses and the awakening I suddenly knew that this long-heralded book had nearly formed itself. I would soon be brought to term. Constance would insist. We did as all lovers do, we hid. I did not want you looking over my shoulder. Hence I sent out an inaccurate account of our whereabouts. The silence and the heat were a wonderful backcloth to our loving, while in the evening the gipsies came, or Sabine alone. They brought us a flock of white-manes, the chargers of heaven, with all the runaway tilt of Schubert impromptus, immaculate as our kisses. On horseback we set out across the network of dykes and canals and lakes; into a mauve desert sunset, with a silent Sabine in between us who had much to tell those who asked the right questions. (Man is the earth quantity and woman the sky: man mind, woman intuition.) Several times now I recognised that I nearly died of love in the night for my heart stopped for appreciable lapses of time and I felt myself entering the penumbra of the continuum, to hover for a long while in an unemphatic state of mystical contingency! Genius is silence, everybody knows that. But who can attain it? With every orgasm you drown a little in the future, taste a little immortality despite yourself. And here I was hoping not only to tell the truth but also to free the novel a bit from the shackles of causality with a narrative apparently dislocated and disjointed yet informed by mutually contradictory insights – love at first insight, so to speak, between Constance and myself. An impossible task you always tell me, but the higher the risk the greater the promise! That is the heart of the human paradox. I did not want to fuck her at first, I did not *dare* to want to because there was so much as yet unrehearsed and unrealised between us. And it might never have been brought to book, so to speak, had it not been for touch – for her probing massage of my wounded back, for while her hands were modelling the repair of the flesh we often spoke of the past, and one day she confessed that she had always been in love with me! 'From the first look we exchanged on the slip at Lyons as we set off down the Rhône. But alas!' Alas indeed, for I was completely unfledged, completely cowardly, if only because I realised the import-ance of that look but could not believe that it meant anything to her. But my adoration must have sunk into her, for all our subsequent lives, the long detour we made, was informed by the force of that single look! Old Shakes was right – or rather Chris Marlowe. Whoever loved that loved not at first sight? And I was glad retrospectively that I had waited on the event in full cowardice and inexperience rather than risk spoiling it by a *gaffe*, for she too had been physically inexperienced, though of course psychically fully mature and aware of the dilemma. What a calamity ignorance is. And with the war and its separations hovering over us. You have no hold over destiny when you are young. How much better to wait. An enigma is more than a mere puzzle – and a premature marriage can become just intellectual baby-sitting."

From Sutcliffe's notebook

Femme à déguster	CAUCHEMAR
Mais pas à boire	COUCHEMAR
Homme à délester	CACHEMERE

Mais pas à croire   COCHEMUR

BLAN: "Here on these quiet lagoons or trotting the dusk mauve sands of the Saintes Maries I learned the truth about the significance of love and its making. 'Because fashions have changed, and the woman's freedom is confirmed. She has slipped the hook.' So Sabine says riding coolly and thoughtfully between us by the rustling sea, 'And now the new lovers will become at last philosophers. They will realise themselves in mating and sharing the orgasm. Nobody will notice that they are dying of loneliness.' "

SUT: "Don Juan, eh? No, Bon Juan the new hero. You will walk about in a muse, looking as if you had had your prostate massaged by leprechauns. And when you die you will go straight to the Poets' Corner of the Abbey. They will write on your plaque: 'Aubrey was not always his own best friend and sometimes got into intellectual positions his enemies could not have wished for more. Finally, exhausted with so much realising, he farted his way to Paradise.' "

As for the book it was a hopeless task, for what is to be done with characters who are all the time trying to exchange selves, turn into each other? And then, ascribing a meaning to point-events? There is no meaning and we falsify the truth about reality in adding one. *The universe is playing, the universe is only improvising!*

Sutcliffe says, "Who knows all this? You should say, in the interests of clarity."

"I leave you to guess."

"Sabine?"

"Yes, walking by the lagoon or in the hot crypt where the bitumen-black waxen figure of Saint Sara stands sending out waves of divination across the fumes of the hot candles. See? There are no sutras, no prayers, no literature to split hairs over. It's just wish to wish, need to need, like spittle falling

on a red-hot iron. You ignite the black doll and she answers
any question that does not concern the past or the future! As
for me, I am a bit of a fraud and an interloper. Why? Because
I joined them out of curiosity – and you can't really. You have
to be born one. So I remained outside, a vehement observer.
History rolls on but the gipsy folk follow an unconscious star
rhythm, they don't take part, they invigilate, so to speak. They
have refused to codify impulse like the Jews, to profiteer.
Now, with the slow breakdown of deterministic Christianity,
one wonders if Nietzsche was not right when he said that the
Jewish role historically was to unlock the gate from the inside
– the ancient intellectual fifth column of radicalism forever at
work with its messianic fanaticism gnawing at the roof-tree
of tradition and stability. Thus they did for the Goths and now
they have done for us. Divide and rue! There is no hint of
illiberality or partiality in these notions which are purely
philosophic. For us gipsies both Hitler and Stalin were children
of the Old Testament executing a blood programme inspired
by Moloch. There is nothing to be done to hasten its inevitable
disappearance and its transformation into something new,
thank goodness! People fall into these thought moulds from
copying each other. But we can with justice accuse Christianity of masterminding our intellectual disarray. As for the
gipsies, they have made no effort to capitalise on the tragedy
of their extermination in the camps as the Jews have done. A
total silence is all that has emerged – not a poem, not a song,
not a scrap of protest folklore! It's uncanny. But the old
aptitudes hold – basketwork, thieving, prophecy and the
telling of fortunes still hold out. The game of destiny."

"Ah! That's what I want to discuss!" said Constance,
"because it all seems a pack of lies. The last time we came
down here we each had different fortunes, each by a different
soothsayer. Surely there must be some constant in the whole
business, Sabine?"

The swarthy woman shook her head and smiled.

"We each have as many destinies stacked up inside us as a melon has seeds. They live on *in potentia* so to speak. One does not know which will mature. But after the event one pretends that it was obvious all along. And sometimes the soothsayer is right, chooses right, skries the destiny which manifests itself! You have many discernible destinies – in one you are to die in childbirth; Aubrey divined this though he is no soothsayer, and it figures in the first draft of his novel. In another you will die together – this our tribal Mother saw. It is part of a great accident, something like an earthquake. All of you, all of us, have as many destinies as the sands of the seashore.

"But as for you, Aubrey, I saw something else of more immediate experience. Suddenly she has discovered in you the love she feared would never exist, since there seemed no hope of you ever snapping out of your coma. Suddenly she realised that if she staked her claim and risked everything you might get reborn, re-created. It was up to her to divine the meaning of the orgasm with complete female ruthlessness, to divine your metaphysical anguish, and then to respond to it – to yield and to conceive, that is what she is trying to do. You have both realised love as a future-manufacturing yoga with a child at stake in it, the consciousness of a child, which will be read in its regard! You know the old Provençal saying that a child anyone can make, but one must *round off or perfect its regard* (*faut parfaire le regard*). This hints at the inner vision which will give the child a pithy heart and mind on condition that the dual orgasm is experienced simultaneously. She is going to rescue you!"

It certainly felt like that, though poor Constance, responding to the analyst in her, explained it all quite differently, indeed somewhat apologetically. "I am at the moment taking the male part, overwhelming you, almost I am castrating you, but the intention is finally to cause you to respond fully to me. You see you are still traumatised by the shock of the explosion and your image of your body is making you mentally cringe, as if you had pain to fear; whereas I know now that the wound is healed and while there are some muscular movements you can't make there is no more pain or stress. You can go the whole hog and act without thinking or hesitating. Last night I felt you for the first time in control. Sabine is right, we are moving into a fine dual control of the act." Yet he knew they had Affad to thank for much of this love-lore.

SAB: "Yes, there are precautions to be taken just as in the making of bread! By progressively conquering the loving amnesia of the orgasm and expanding its area of consciousness – adding more and more meaning to the eyes of the child-future. By this voluntary extension of consciousness you refine your death progressively, the death he will inherit from you. Once you start this process and realise fully what you are doing all stress vanishes, and all unbelief also. You become all of a sudden who you are, thanks to her, and she who she is thanks to you! But you must not make it sound too like a *constatation de gendarme* or Sutcliffe will be forced to redress the balance in his notebooks which presumably will be one day inherited by Trash. All these pitiful slogans of desire! (After intercourse show him amazement – advice to young brides.)"

But how to overpraise the gold body of Constance, dusted now by the dust-thunder of the bullrings and splashed with freckles of gold?

> Sweet as a rock-panther one day old
> Just come on heat and mateless
> Melts like a cat in rut unsated
> In vast desires unsublimated
> Freckles of coy gold . . .

BLAN: "Why should death have the monopoly, eh? *Il faut paufiner la réalité, faut bricoler dans l'immédiat!* Why remain a victim of uncouth wishes? As for love among the martial arts you must read my new study of Cleopatra, to learn the secrets of love from her. She buttered her breasts before intercourse while Antony honeyed his valves! Soft probe of human tongue – hysteria is a distress which does not come from blameless kisses exchanged between male and female adversaries. The new lovers have become philosophers and equal to the loneliness they inspire. The tremendous sadness becomes rich though the love seems profitless. *Something quite new is happening!*"

These philosophic considerations sound highly sententious, and one suspects that too many of them could easily spoil your loving to the tune of this lazy night and this quite momentous sleek jazz pouring up among the lamplit trees. Can't you be content with the soft goads of the simple flesh? Of that wonderful girl Blanford invented he wrote in his book: "Her husbands had tried to ring her like a wild swan but she was subject only to the gravitational tides of the seasons, flying north or south where the blood called, eluding settled ways and settled men. In lonely places I always found her, tide-borne, solitary, perfect, my lover and my deep friend. At night we dined by the light of a single candle, with olives and iced wine."

BLAN: "When Sutcliffe was born it was a time of grave portents. The doctor said, 'It is clear he will die young for he has no sense of humour.' But his French nurse (muse?) leaned over his cot and whispered, 'They have all brought gifts as spurs to the crib, Zeus a garlic-squeezer, Venus a foreskin-clip of purest gold portending loves without drawback. And now think: the white breast of chicken musky with dusky truffles, stippled like a trout's belly: a pot of black aromatic olives dense in the sweet introspection of their own dark oil, *pâté de foie gras.* Admit it, my dear, you are getting an erection!' The *démon du Midi* has him by the hair of a Sunday.

> Aborted Christians drinking blood
> A thirst which dates before the Flood.
> I'm sick of the thirst for becoming,
> The heaving and retching and humming,
> I will turn to a thirst to exist
> And catch up on all that I've missed!''

The private mind is never at rest, and always on the magic frequency of love.

SUT: "The formula seems to be *petit talent et gros cul.* Fond as a stableful of horses' bums polished up to mirror grooms' grins. They burn. They burn. But nowadays you must bring your own whip. But this is how the gentry do it. With us and our little white palaeolithic chargers it is quite different, for they behave like pets and live loose on the range when they are unsaddled, prodigal of their smiles and head-long tossing of white manes, as if they had leaped out of context and no longer respected the serial order expounded by nature. Think: old men's sperm makes not old men but infants-in-arms who will grow to form church fathers sim-mering in the raging paranoia of a punitive God. A thirst for magic rules. The schizoid states are uncrystallised mysticism. The kundalini of the unconscious accidentally touched off and set in motion, like an engine's pre-ignition; it comes from incautious thinking, incautious wishing."

BLAN: "Art for the Prince is the representation of a reality upon a plane surface – an artefact without volume or depth. It will not stand up to interrogation. You risk by poking at it with your questions to go right through the canvas into nothing: or else everything! There are limits even to everything. *Bien sûr que non,* as you can say in French, using the cryptic Buddhic double negative. As for the woman, she is a psychic scout and pathfinder through the flesh, a lieutenant, the ship's first mate who divides responsibility with the captain."

When the Prince overheard Constance say, "We have started getting a poor quality of human being for whom wisdom has become mere information!" he was entranced and begged her to teach him ethnology. Together they frequented international gatherings and wistfully compared cultures in search of a thread of historic significance. Certain symbols stood out and seemed to hint. The suffering Prometheus, for example, stood with its face to the rock while the vultures fluttered and pecked; while the suffering Christian stood with its back to the cross, arms spread like a radio aerial, with a crown of wild acacia on his head . . . Two different approaches to human suffering! A professor had said, "The will to self-destruction seems more advanced in the more gifted nations or peoples." The Prince gave an exclamation of impatience, for he had begun to feel that they would never find what they were looking for in this way. Also the fortune-tellers had predicted the death of the Princess, and he had begun to dream of the funeral cortège – the long procession of Rolls-Royces, nose to stern, stretching some eighteen kilometres along the blazing desert road between Cairo and Alexandria. The screeching water wheels of Egypt are the country's cicadas. He would soon have to return to her, the one being without whom he did not think he could continue to live. "*C'est une affaire de tangences*," somebody had remarked to him in the midst of a cocktail party on the Lake Mareotis. And now that the thought of her dying had become an echo in his mind how boring all other women seemed, how shabby his sprees! They were tergiversatile and showed him their lily-white panjandrums, that was all! (The value of the hypotenuse of the Pythagorean triangle is valued at five!) Yet he must not be unfair. With some he had learned things which profited his love for his own wife, and in one – why, she had opened her legs and revealed the whole secret of the pyramids and, yes, that of entropy also. But there is also a principle of repair which contests the irreversibility of process for a short spell – the omnifact of omnideath, the ubique of human obsolescence. "I want you to go ahead and try out the child, one of your own, it's a great challenge," he said to Constance, who replied in somewhat oracular fashion, "Even though you know full well that lovers are selfish as arrows?"

"Even though! Even though!"

Blanford took her in his arms, which was still an unfamiliar purchase for the two unfledged hearts, unquiet presences. He said ironically, "With this future I thee wed." But they knew that the trick had long since been done and it only remained to live it out, to act it out. Reality is desperate for someone to believe in it; hence manifestation which is History's party frock!

> Dull carnivorous males in love
> A-playing the game of hand-in-glove;
> Projections of our self-esteem
> Reflected into love's young dream.
> Gonads rehearse the Primal Scream
> Man, sublime mud of all he thinks
> Sleepwalks in darkness with his jinx,
> Gaunt fellatrix with urban curves,
> Each gets the partner he deserves.

SUT: "Passing down the village street they were reflected in the shop windows, the three mounted figures; the gold leaf of her sunburn glowed against the blonde head like a declaration of intent. Living without awe is living without a full consciousness of reality – of its value. Men without awe will never be wise. Ah! for men who realise that reality consistently outstrips intellectual formulations. Sometimes we could not help seeing the world as a sort of farmyard – with

humanity quacking or honking rather than talking. Ontology
– the study of being! Ours is perhaps the first civilisation
which cannot decide if the answers lie in art or in science.
They appear to flow from different centres in the same animal,
man. And a man now must realise himself through a sort of
religious experience yet stay a man. But if a woman has a
religious experience she is obliged to forsake her womanhood
and become a nun. Can you have the grin without the cat? I
am not sure. A suicide wrote recently, 'In leaving you I am
inheriting the whole world!' For dinner he had eaten lobsters
tender as Christian children and an overloaded conscience is as
bad as an overloaded bowel – something has to give! Then
bang!"

They had started to make love as if their embraces were
extensions of their thoughts, and he realised the full extent
of her power over him; it was a little frightening because he
realised that later he would be called upon to take over this
power, this domination – it belonged to the male demesne.
She was only trying to waken him to his responsibilities. They
hardly talked now. The long silent rides were wonderfully
tonic beside bulky seas. And their little tavern was as abomin-
able as ever, serving slices of ancient donkey badly cooked
and served tepid, covered in rancid oil. The tavern should
have been called the Bloodstained Toothpick instead of the
Mistral. The proprietor had the specially dead look you see
in the eyes of a fly. One knew it was no use arguing because
he did not understand. Yet the wine was marvellous. It came
from St Saturnin. Suddenly one had thoughts of pith. "*Oui,
en toi j'ai bien vendangé ma mère!*" he told her. It was a
declaration of love of the most absolute kind and she recognised it as such, good Freudian that she was, or seemed!

So they rode in sweet symbiosis, while the ravenous blue
sea lopped at the land, honed down their horizons of sand,
extended its bony contours cradled by the heartfelt blue

meniscus which was sky. She had finally convinced him of the existence of lovers as philosophers, and of the need for a joint approach to time through the atom of their love. And this sometimes made them both a bit of a bore. "For me the *Aetiologie of Hysteria* is the great document of the twentieth century, the great Sutra, so to speak, and the Freudian denial of its truth is quite inexplicable; it is as momentous as the other great philosophic denial ('Thou shalt deny me thrice!') which ended with the crucifixion scene." What she meant was that the child would be clear-eyed and vigorous and unshocked in its beginnings – she knew it must be so. On the other hand . . . "I had this *dream* which suggested that it was going to be the ending of the whole book. You went back to Tu Duc to tidy up and I to England in order most appropriately to begin my opus. And there the telephone rang with news of your . . . I have never accepted the unique word." "Say it!" "No! It must be lived to be swallowed!"

Death!

BLAN: "Your consciousness bears witness to the historic *now* which you are living while your memory recalls other nows, fading slowly into indistinctness as they move into the prehistory you call the *past*. This temporal series, indistinct and overlapping, you attach to one individual whom you call 'I'. But . . . in the course of a few years, about seven I think, every cell in the body of this 'I', this individual, has been modified and even replaced. His thoughts, judgements, emotions, desires have all undergone a similar metamorphosis! What then is the permanence which you designate as an 'I'? Surely not simply a name which marks his ('its'?) difference from his ('its?') fellow men . . . A discrete sequence of rather disjointed recollections which begin some time in infancy and terminate with a jolt *now*, in the *present* – such is time as a datum of consciousness! (Despite this stone wall, I love you more than myself!) When all this raw material has undergone

the strange refining process which we know as physical
intuition it is transformed into something close to a meditative
state – a version of 'calm abiding' as the Tibetans would say,
and it becomes an ark or house for the love-child to inhabit,
afloat upon the waters of the eternal darkness, backcloth of
everything we do or every kiss we exchange. When if ever
one has the luck to arrive at an inferential consciousness the
steps of the reasoning process that preceded it are no longer
necessary; one can let them go! Kick away the ladder, so to
speak."

> Sutcliffe will write us epitaphs
> In poems acerb and wise
> In rhythms the pendulums adore
> And human metronomes despise.

Constance turned her smiling head and sighed: "You
have not seen as much of death as I have in my work. Finally,
I have got on to good terms with the ugly fellow! Somewhere
in the middle of the whole thing there comes a sudden
luxurious feeling of surrender to inevitability in the dying
themselves. It belongs, this mood of gradually deepening
amnesia, to the rhythms of plant life. It makes one realise that
all love passes into obsolescence in the very act – it illustrates
the nothingness we have decorated with our trashy narcissism.
A soft withering surrender to a death without throes. Lying
alone by oneself there guided by the merciful paralysis of
fading thoughts which cradle one and lead on and on and on
. . . until snap! Kiss me. Hold me. And then for some time the
echo of an emptiness will follow you about the house,
invisible as gravity but as omnipresent, the emphasis on a
vanished presence."

Yes, Rob's poems will come all tension-charged with the
original perfect illness to undo our knots and make us thrive
on images of unimpeded loves . . . He knows that the flesh cools

also like a pot of clay in freshly ovened silence, set out in gardens like women beautiful and purposeless as fruit but just as suave in their archaic silence as the grave.

> Faustus who held all nature in contempt
> Was punished, could not die,
> Instead he went
> Into the limbo of the death-exempt,
> Becoming everything he might have dreamt.

To him was granted the famous penis with three heads – the Noble Toy of the alchemists. From now on they made love, creaking like old tennis racquets, and he was able to note in his diary that "*le temps du monde fini a commencé*".

I have made a discovery but I can't tell you what it is because the language in which to express it has not been invented. I know a place but there is no road to it – you must swim or fly – thus the mage Faustus. What's to be done? Why, we must push on with reality, living in the margins of hope.

> the puckering of a thousand vaginas
> the groans and squeaks of minors
> the booming of ocean liners
> the sighs of aircraft designers
> the concentrations of water diviners
> well blow me down with mortal slyness!
> tickle my arse and call me Chomsky!

The adjective which is the prop of good prose is the perverter of poetry – except in the limerick which is its proper show-window. Ideally one could write a whole book in this concise and convenient form to sidestep memory's slow ooze, though perhaps the too rigorous beat of the metronome might lead to monotony. In slower prose one can let packets of silence drift about like mist. Truth is not only stranger but older than . . . The whole of reality dreamed up by a shaggy little god muttering in his sleep. *Eppur si muove!* He talks as if he needed hot rivets to clench up his prose – yes, aphorisms like rivets!

> Let him who writes with velvet nib
> Reserve a sigh for Women's Lib
> Confusions Imp, the God of Love
> Must ask them what they are dreaming of.

SUT: "Darling, soon they will abolish the male and you will have to consider joining the Sperm Bank, the most select form of civil servant, with a certain guaranteed sperm-count, and a uniform like a treasury official. They wear their gold chain of office proudly, simply. And the girls sigh after them – those who have only known the ministrations of the homely plastic syringe torn from a steel dispenser, the dose kept at blood heat, but often not quite fresh or even out of date. Oh for a real man, a small beef extract of a man to enliven the Effluent Society presided over by Madame Ovary. The taming of the screw.

"God's brush!" he cried, "with every lady kissed
The future is encouraged to exist!"

"Constance, you overpersuade me – perhaps we are the last specimens of an obsolete cult. (Cuddle the embers of memory and she'll be thine – so I tell myself.) All is not lost. I sit on the nursery floor of literature surrounded by the dismembered fragments of my juggernaut of a book, wondering how best to assemble this smashed telamon. The débris itself gives off light despite its incoherence. Some wise and disciplined girl like you with those inevitable eyes in shadow, disgusted by the petty transactions of time, suddenly finds plain love and its choice delights; so crowding on all sail she heads for the dark fronts where the great attachments hide. In the heart of the licensed confusion a sense of meaning. All beak and virgin's claws in girls of renown. Or in old men whose basic valves have shut; despairing silence holds them yet, though all but their earthly sun is set . . . And love's umbilicus is cut. Neurosis is the norm for an egopetal culture – Freud exposed the roots as a dentist's drill exposes the pulp chamber of a tooth – the aching root is guilt over uncommitted sins! Civilisation is a placebo with side-effects."

They made love again, secure in this despairing knowledge of a truth their embraces exemplified!

EIGHT

Minisatyrikon

"IT WAS PURE ROMAN SWANK, IF YOU ASK ME," SAID LORD Galen comfortably. "When you think that the whole of this huge edifice was brought into being just to convey a current of fresh water twenty-five kilometres away to a waterless Nîmes where the eleventh legion had been sent in as settlers . . . pure swank, that's what it was." They were taking a turn upon the bridge in the fading light, waiting for the festivities to begin, for at long last the great day had arrived for the unveiling of the Templar treasure in the caves. "Perhaps," said Felix Chatto who had joined the strollers in the dusk, "perhaps," as he gazed upwards into the evening sky where the felicitous honey-golden arches rose in an unpretentious explicitness, "it didn't represent very much for their architects – a mere hydraulic work, inescapably functional. Not even a Roman virgin bricked up alive in it as a sacrifice to the goddess of water!" The Prince nodded and added, "As far as we know! But could it not have been to create employment and prevent social discontent, and thus to ingratiate the Roman settlers with their hosts? Surely it was not just showing off, eh? It's exasperating that one doesn't know. Nor do we know at what point a purely functional object, a fort, a railway, a dam, becomes suddenly (as if by a change of key) aesthetically precious." It was not perhaps the place and the time for such aesthetic promptings, for since the prefectorial announcement of a festival and *vin d'honneur* in honour of the reconstituted niche of Saint Sara the gipsies had taken the hint and started to invade the valley with its tall cliffs and dense forest land which cradled the green river and its fast variable currents lapping at the stone-shingle beaches.

"We'll never discover," said Felix with a sigh. "Many years ago we discovered a Greek monastery with a juke box in it and were carried away by the charm of the unusual in such a remote place. One of the monks had visited America and brought back this cultural object as an *ex voto*. It was delightful and quite incongruous. Several years later we returned to discover that every monastery on the peninsula had one if not more juke boxes which played canned music all day long at full volume. The singular and charming had become the horrible. How was it? Is the good, the desirable, the admirable, dependent on its rareness and vitiated by quantity? I have often wondered." Lord Galen felt unhappy, out of his depth. He knew he had little talent for Aristotelean casuistries. "Surely," he ventured, "more is better than less, as with money?"

Felix shook his head.

"Or bacteria?"

"Oh dear!" said Lord Galen, "I hate this line of reasoning because it never seems to lead anywhere. Would you feel it was a bad thing if Greek monasteries invested more in sanitary equipment? Myself, I should feel it admirable."

But while this pious wrangling went on in good-natured fashion Sutcliffe was noting in his commonplace-book the salient facts about the place and time – this might serve Aubrey if for some reason he did not turn up or was late, or whatever. The basic thing was that all the visitants, of whatever persuasion, were expecting something different from the adventure. For the Prince and his associates material gain, for the Beaux Arts aesthetic, for the gipsies a prophesying oracle, and so on. Even the little doctor and the egregious Quatrefages with his strange epileptoid air and cadaverous physique were expecting something in the nature of a revelation about the Templar *mystique*, the Templar secret. All these matters would come to a head – with any luck – after midnight when the revellers would be led away from the scene of the festivities towards the dark quarries with their labyrinth of grottoes. As for the gipsies, they knew how to do things with subtlety, to penetrate by infiltration, cart by cart, tribe by tribe. The magic word had been uttered and passed along the blood-stream of the race so that tribes from as far away as the northern Balkans, from Yugoslavia, from Italy and Algeria, had found that there was just sufficient time in hand to send a few representatives to this important event which in the gipsy tongue was known as "an awakening" – that is to say, the inauguration of a tribal saint, a soothsayer and initiator. It was natural that the tribes in and around the city should be pre-eminent as being numerically the most important, and most closely in touch with the authorities. They smoothed out difficulties with the police and the various other depart-ments concerned with public events. So far all the organisa-tional side had been worked out with precision and aimi-ability, though as for the Préfet himself he had passed a sleepless night, for in the middle of it he had awoken from his sleep with a start and a chilly shudder of fright – for he had suddenly realised the fearful fire hazard which the surrounding forest created at the Pont du Gard. And here he had even authorised a brief display of *fireworks* to salute the risen Saint Sara! His blood ran cold as he realised all that might go wrong . . . a single imprudence by a smoker, an overturned lamp . . . With a vague if scared sense of propitiation he rose early that morning and went to mass, but throughout was preoccupied with visions of a Pont du Gard in flames. It was too late to change anything but he called for the fire brigade to send out a strategic work force just in case . . .

But nevertheless the whole event had been regarded as a municipal operation of some importance to the town of Avignon (to flatter gipsy pride) and it was envisaged that the whole hamlet and ravine would be occupied by sightseers and participants during the fête. The town *pompiers* had taken the matter in hand with despatch, beginning with the problem of lighting. Wires had been slung across the gulf with ribbons of coloured bulbs suspended from them, worked off a portable generator in a lorry, so for the first time the whole edifice was lit up against the night sky. This was in addition to its own lighting system which it was able to use on national days and events of a tourist sort. This whole area of swinging illumination created a sort of mesmeric village of light scooped out of the theatrical blue darkness of the night sky. On either side the cliffs mounted with their dense scrub and forests of holm oak, and here the gipsy bands had already taken root. (The blood chilled, for one could not prevent them from lighting small fires on the embers of which they grilled their evening meal!) They had brought all their own equipment with them, trade by trade, tongue by tongue; they travelled in ancient lorries or in slower carts with their verminous armfuls of keen-eyed children. They had even brought their own fleas with them, if one was to believe the municipal police on the subject! And then there was their music which, once the occupation of the site got under way, began to proliferate in a variety of styles and modes with different groups of instruments and differently cadenced songs and airs – whining mandolins purring like cats, quailing ailing violins, trombones like village idiots reciting their themes. And then to follow came the dances of the children. And as this invasion advanced the place was steadily filling up with little stalls where one could buy pasties or roasted meat dishes or fruit or scones, or even trinkets and baskets – fruit of the day-labour of the gipsies, for they neglected no chance to foster their wares. And here, manning other stalls, were farriers who could shoe you a horse or key-cutters who could cut you a set of skeleton keys to open an office safe or knifegrinders who could sharpen your kitchen knives in a flash. And sellers of scarves and lace and brilliant coloured napkins from Turkey or Yugoslavia. And lastly the army of fortune tellers, brilliant as parrots and all professing palmistry . . .

Meanwhile a central marquee had been run up, extensive as to size, for it was to house most of the notables and provide a centre inside which the Préfet could made his speech in honour of Saint Sara. He never missed the chance of speechifying in public. It was his job as well as his art.

The nexus of the gipsy organisation was centred in half a dozen old fashioned carts with small windows decorated by brilliant curtains and flashily painted sideboards. They were grouped about the loftiest and most gaudy which was the home of the tribal "Mother". The smell of joss and whisky hung about in it, to tantalise the noses of those clients who came to consult the old lady about their fortunes. All this smoke from fires and tobacco and cooking and Indian joss-sticks ebbed and flowed with the evening river-winds as they poured softly over the stony sills of the ravines and so downstream.

"I'm on the look-out for that Sabine lady," said Lord Galen, "to try to get a really detailed and authoritative reading out of her. She was rather unsatisfactory last time when we went to the Saintes Maries; and yet there was sufficient truth in what she said to be very striking, and give me the hunger to know more if possible."

"Did she tell you if you would get the treasure?" asked the Prince curiously. "No! I thought not. Nor me exactly! But she defended her limitations very ably, I thought, by saying that she could only see what lay within her personal competence, just as a human eye can only see a certain distance. Yet I was like you impressed by what she had to say."

Felix Chatto who had decided to resign everything to fate and had a poor opinion of fortune telling was nevertheless just as anxious to see Sabine whom he admired deeply and thoroughly appreciated as a conversationalist. He had himself grown up so much and in so many unexpected ways that he felt the need to test out his new maturity upon someone whose sensibility seemed to be the equal of his own, whose notions echoed his. And he could see that the woman was hungry for good conversation in her own tongue which offered her the comforting support of humour and lightness of touch. But where was she? She did not reach the great viaduct until nightfall, owing to some minor trouble with the transport. She had lost a very great deal of weight within the last year or two – indeed, she already knew that she was starting a cancer; but for the moment she had gained much in simple beauty which she could offset with the dramatic apparel of the gipsy tribe in all its brilliant grossness; and her body answered the change, reverting to the old swinging walk of the past, her head slanted to one side, as if she were listening to her own beauty from some inward point of vantage. They heard her hoarse voice in the crowd and exclaimed (or Galen did): "There she is! Let's waylay her before she gets carried away by the French Préfet!"

Meet they did, but it seemed that Sabine had been on the lookout for Felix, for she advanced upon them with impulsive speed and took his hands, ignoring the arms of Galen, keen to share a handshake with her. "I must talk to you alone for a moment," she said breathlessly, "if your friends will permit me. I have something to tell you." And so saying she drew him aside into the forest and sat him down on a fallen block of golden stone, an ingot broken off the bridge. "When we spoke of Sylvie I did not tell you the whole of what I saw because I realised that there was something capital which you did not yet understand, and that was the provisional nature of prophesy. The fact that I see something does not automatically mean that it will come about, for sometimes it does not; yet statistically it falls out as I see it about seven times out of ten. You questioned me about her illness and her possible death by suicide and I turned the question aside at the time. I wanted time to consult my Mother as to what I had a right to reveal and what not – for I saw quite far into your future, or my version of it. In that version she does not die that way, but she is buried alive in a mountainous snowdrift somewhere north of Zagreb some years off, some years from now. In between you will experience absolute bliss with her, for you have, by recognising the nature of her so-called illness, given her the courage to reassume her reason. As a young Ambassador I see health and riches and professional success. But this catastrophe comes quite unexpectedly. They are there silent; the uniformed chauffeur is dozing. They are waiting for help to come in order to dig them out. She is playing chess with a pocket chess set. I hear Smoke, the cat, purring contentedly and also the soft tick of the dashboard clock of the great limousine. Help will come, but too late; the rescue team have laboriously dug a tunnel down to the bottom of the drift to remove the bodies but the car is jammed in rocks and incapable of being moved. It will have to stay all winter and wait for the spring thaw. By then of course the moisture will have blurred the contents of her last two note-books – a great loss to literature, they seem to believe." All this while holding his wrist and staring down at his palm with a trance-like expression. Then she sighed. "That is all. And now you must please excuse me for a few moments because I think the French have arrived."

Indeed the French had arrived; that is to say that repre-sentatives of the Press with their cameras had already started to put in an appearance, reassured by the promise offered by the more than adequate buffet which was still only halfway mounted. This creation had been confided to the great chef of Nîmes, Tortoni, who amidst a multiplicity of highly comestible cakes and pâtés had prepared the pedestal for the most important of his creations, a recumbent woman fashioned in butter with trimmings uttered in caviar of several different provenances and helpings of *saumon fumé* and an archipelago of iced potato salad to round out the offering. Venus rising from a Récamier of Baltic caviar with the smile of a redeemer on her lovely face, just to remind everyone that Tortoni had attended Les Arts before turning aside into a career as a gastronomic chef which had brought him fame and fortune. But all this superlative invention had to be kept chilled and here again great ingenuity came into play, for the whole creation was offered in a disguised thermal showcase upheld by captious looking Cupids with sweet erections and honeyed grins. "I must say," said Galen proudly, "you really do have good ideas sometimes." For it was the Prince who had thought up this little gastronomic frolic, as the Préfet's budget for such a feast was somewhat cheese-paring. "I only hope it wasn't too expensive," he added, for the Prince in his lordly way had sent the bill to the company. He shook his head reproachfully and said, "Ah! you and your money! I dreamed last night that you died and were incinerated and that your ashes were scattered over your bank in Geneva by helicopter." Galen laughed heartily: "And that you built a funerary memorial in the crypt of the bank itself!"

But Galen's mirth was superseded by a thoughtful look, as if in afterthought the idea didn't sound too unreasonable! The Prince continued on his mischievous teasing way: "I remembered Voltaire's advice to people visiting Geneva and wondered if you knew it." Galen did not, so the Prince obligingly repeated it: "Voltaire said, 'When you visit Geneva, if you see a banker jump out of a third-storey window jump after him. There will be three per cent in it!' " This put Galen in a thoroughly good humour. "Old Banquo used to say that if you put your ear to a Geneva bank you could hear it purring just like a Persian cat. The noise was the discreet noise of the interest on capital accruing!" Felix clicked his tongue reprovingly at so much flippancy, but he was only pretending to disapprove. The Prince said, "Admit it, Felix. It's a Mouton-Rothschild world with far too little merriment in it. As for me I'm dying to plunge my spoon into the buttery buttocks of the Tortoni Venus; but I think we will have to wait for the Préfet, no?"

Obviously they would have to, in the interests of correct protocol as well as a sense of occasion; but of course it was obvious that the gipsies themselves could only be allowed a limited share in this upper-class celebration. Though it was in their honour they seemed to accept the fact with equanimity. The Préfet's congratulatory speech had been copied and its distribution to the Press Corps achieved; its actual construction had proved something of a puzzle for he saw that it would have to be written in a manner which suggested that the statue had been in fact found – yet delivered before the fact, so to speak! It contented itself with expressing itself on a warm note of benevolence and goodwill – turns of phrase habitual enough in speeches of an official kind. But the actual gipsy participation was of a limited kind inside the official marquee, though in fact they completely dominated the musical fête which had grown up around the events: already the smoke from the flares and the lights and plangence of the music provided a wild note of romantic colour, a felicity and unbridled expansiveness to the proceedings which was reminiscent of other more important gipsy rejoicings – such as the one in honour of the original Saint Sara at the Saintes Maries de la Mer at the end of May every year. So much colour to delight the eye that Sutcliffe was drunk prematurely, without the ever-present aid of wine. He had asked Sabine if she would consider sleeping with him, and she had looked at him for a long time in a very strange manner. "But I don't know which one of you is more real – for Aubrey has already asked me that." To which Rob testily replied, "Is one not permitted a practising *alter ego* in the modern world? I am the ape-carrier of tradition, for in great houses the Fool customarily carried his Lord's ape! Why all the mystery? When you are writing from the hither side of a deeply privileged experience a certain hilarity is quite in order if only to express your elation. That is why I love you, for you have realised that as far as individual identity is concerned we only give an illusion of coherence. Your I, me, mine, has about as much consistency as a vapour. Sabine, I am turning into a rainbow! I can feel it. Slowly but gracefully. I am full of love and mis-giving for I have learned how to write poems. There comes a struggle, a feeling of suffocation, an agon, a convulsion – before you can take that vital step forward into the unknown! I want to escape from time through the perfect amnesia of the orgasm. Time! Have you not noticed how much one second resembles another? All time is but a uniform flow of process. It is *we* who age and disappear!"

"Come to my caravan," she said. It was an order.

But though they had not advanced upon the food they had started to broach the champagne, and were beginning to enjoy the twinges of elation it brought. Flash bulbs began to pop off and everyone began to feel that he was about to be immortalised. And the music soared together with the general conversation which had reached the pitch of coherence common to cocktail parties – as if a whole collective un-conscious had like a wine-bowl been overturned. Galen was saying: "You scared me so much with your talk of serpents and buried treasure – the Egyptian folk stories, remember? – that I bought myself a stout stick with a steel spike atop, and I shall take it with me just in case." The Prince chuckled: "How typical!" he said, "when the real danger is of stepping on a mine!" New arrivals began to put in an appearance, like the doctor Jourdain and the saturnine Quatrefages and even (surprisingly) Max, looking even more like God-the-Father than ever: it was as if the very spirit of old age had come to nest, to find its apotheosis in his white-haired gravity and beauty. Galen had paid for him to be present, since he also had been created a sleeping partner in the company. "What has happened to Constance?" he wanted to know, and was delighted when Felix replied: "The best and the worst! She has fallen in love with Aubrey and disappeared. But they promised to appear tonight for the ceremony so perhaps we shall see them here before long." The old man bowed his head. He was thinking to himself, "Love not disembodied must end in despair and forgiveness. One will ask oneself if that is all that life has to offer. But life has its own imperatives and everything must take its turn. So she was perfectly right to behave as she must. The only art to be learned was how to cooperate with reality and the inevitable!" And then immediately he reproached himself for this rather specious formulation, but at the same time he recognised that it came out of his yoga practice – the fidelity to insight and to oxygen! Nevertheless he was dying to see Constance again and hoped that he would be able to stay awake to talk to her; recently (and regretfully) he had fallen into the habit of dropping off to sleep in a quite involuntary manner after dinner, an annoying symptom of old age against which he was quite powerless!

The Préfet according to his rank was entitled to three kettle-drums for public appearances of importance, but out of modesty he only convoked two for this cultural manifestation. It was almost the only way of subduing a rowdy Mediterranean crowd, of announcing your presence, or making it clear that what you were about to say was supremely important, because official. Kettle-drums create the required hush before a public speech!

Tonight, however, he was possessed by a pleasant

fancy – of descending from his official car and effecting the
last few hundred yards to the bridge on foot, preceded by his
drummers. And this he succeeded in doing, walking at a calm
unhurried pace, clad in his frock-coat with decorations
proudly mounted. The drummers walked before him,
uttering their deep rallentando to mark the step; and as he
advanced the gipsies espied him and made way for his advent,
orienting their music in a manner of speaking towards a
welcoming demeanour. Meanwhile the experienced eye of the
official ran over the scene taking everything in – above all to
see if the leaders of the gipsy tribe were seated correctly in
consonance with that invisible and inscrutable element,
protocol. He was reassured to see that the old lady, the
"Mother" of the tribe, who looked rather the worse for wear
already, had been planted firmly at a side table which adjoined
the main one, with her implacable bottle of gin before her, and
some lighted joss to keep things savoury. Her husband and a
whole tribe of sons kept her company, though they were a
tiny bit ill at ease because of the light and the signs of
"officialdom": yet manifestly flattered also. The Préfet made
a slow official circuit now to shake the hands of the invitees,
noting with interest that some of them came from other time-
fields or other contingent realities – like Toby and Drexel,
who was there with his two charming and juvenile *ogres* who
seemed rather like impersonations of Piers and Sylvie of the
past. In fact there was hardly anyone missing except for the
two lovers who were still acting out the long detour of their
age – the biography of that first look exchanged on the river
bank at Lyons so many years ago!

The official presence now authorised the official arc-
lamps of the shrine, and suddenly it was possible to admire
the magnificent presence of the whole monument pressed up
against the sky and coloured by the white arcs in all its
perfectly proportioned grace. No, it was not possible to dis-

miss it as an adequate piece of Roman plumbing, thought Felix as he gazed at it with newly kindled emotions. It raised once again the old tormenting problem. (Beautiful is valuable against Beautiful is precious – which?) It was a question of market value against aesthetic or spiritual value. Max at his elbow spoke as if he had read his thoughts for he said, "No. It's full of spirituality; you could do a very good yoga here and it would be appropriate enough!"

The wine had done its work, the music exercised its charm, the leafy shadow and white light had expressed all the ample beauty of a late spring; and then to crown it all they stood to gain fortunes tonight and to revive the memorable saint who for years now had been forgotten. The roving and curious eye of the Préfet quested about for a moment, he was on the lookout for someone. Presently she came into view and threaded her way through the crowd to his side; it was Sabine, and he was obviously waiting for her. In her deep voice she said, "Monsieur le Préfet, I have made the inquiries you asked of me and the girl is available, and can come to your residence whenever you wish. Her husband has assured me that she is not ill – I appreciate your concern as so many of these folk have venereal troubles. The only trouble is that he wishes something from you *en contrepartie*, and you may not feel like giving him what he asks for . . ." "Anything, within reason," said the Préfet, who was blushing with pleasure, as the girl in question was a magnificent young bird of paradise – or perhaps more appropriately a golden pheasant. Sabine went on: "He wants the centre stall for the Avignon fairs, the stall which is to the left under the old bastion – stall G." The Préfet groaned: "But everyone wants that stall, it is strategically the best in the town. Very well. I shall speak to the *placier* in that sense and he can take possession of it as from tomorrow. And I hope tomorrow evening the girl will make herself available at about eight o'clock. I can't tell you how grateful I am for your personal intervention on my behalf. Sometimes these things are so hard to arrange when one is an official. Thank you a thousand times." Sabine smiled. One is always in a strong position when one is in need of nothing. But she knew that if ever she needed official help with any scheme she could count on her *piston* with the Préfet, and that was important.

But as yet neither had spoken of what was uppermost in their minds – the question of Julio's embalmed legs. It invested their silence with a kind of pregnant significance for on neither side was the conversation broken off, it simply tapered off into silence, into a pause. She left the official with the onus of referring to the subject. "Of course," he said at last, "I am fully aware of the political significance to the tribe of finding the shrine untouched and in working order. In a sense I am as much concerned as you must be – for my job is to see that nothing troubles good civic order."

"Indeed," she said, looking down at her hands as if the answer to the secret might be hidden in them. "Indeed!"

The official drew a deep breath and plunged. "Have you thought any more about my suggestion concerning the legs?"

"Of course I have."

"I am having repeated offers from the Musée de l'Homme; as you know they want to add the originals to their collection. It seems to be a matter of vital interest to them and I am sure the matter could be arranged without anyone knowing. After all with a pair of plastic copies who would be any the wiser?"

"That is not the question. I quoted them a price for the whole transaction. Will they meet it or not? If they will then I agree from my side. If not, not!" The Préfet coughed behind his hand. "They have agreed to your price," he said and his face broke into a smile. But not hers, there was no corresponding smile on her face. So *this* was the discreditable act she must perform according to the cards – for of course plastic copies could not, would not, conduct the lightning flashes of healing to suppliants! She took the proffered cheque and stared at it with puzzled amaze, dazed by her own behaviour. It was a ritual sacrifice of something, though she did not know of what. And it would lead, as the cards had warned her, to her murder by the tribe – ritual murder by stoning. She shook herself like a sheepdog with sheer disbelief. "What rubbish it all is!" she exclaimed. "Rubbish?" said the Préfet. "It seems a fair price to me for such a thing. It's all superstition anyway, so what are the odds?"

He moved slowly on and left her standing there in amazement wondering if she should tear up the cheque but knowing she would not.

Everything was unrolling in the most satisfactory fashion; an unruffled optimism reigned. It was time now to broach the food, and the official approached the gallant spread with all the ardour and enthusiasm of a true Frenchman who is confronted with something good to eat. It is practically a religious duty to do justice to the fare. And by now everyone had caught the mood, and started to follow suit. Fragments of thoughts and snatches of conversation floated about in the breezy darkness of the Roman treasure. Old relationships between acquaintances who had not met for years renewed themselves. Glasses were raised to Saint Sara, and "*trinc*" became once more the password!

"As for Saint Sara, I don't suppose we shall ever know for certain who she was: the repudiated wife of Pilate, the servant of the Virgin, or some forgotten queen of Egypt, reincarnation of Isis, who once ruled over the Camargue. Perhaps it does not matter except to these swarthy children who so reverently kiss her belly button during the fête." Thus the Prince who was enchanted by the excellence of the food and drink and the manner in which things were shaping.

Twinkling with love-bites Cleopatra came,
Saint Sara had resolved her of all shame,
The belly-button of a virgin's kiss
Transformed her very breathing into bliss.

In the unwinking gold of the candlelight all the brass-work in the little caravan twinkled and flashed. Sabine gazed at the two palms of Rob Sutcliffe, allowing her concentration to sink into them, to founder in them until they seemed to her as transparent as glass. "We will be saved if at all by the Jews coming into a new heritage; the persecuted make mistakes and they once made a false identification of interest on capital with safety; this translated into blood as a kind of alchemical investment plus material usury. There will be other ways of stabilising the finances of state and they will show us a new road." Sutcliffe was clad only in his shirt. In his notebook he had written: "The untouchable dreams of licit caresses." He had asked her to marry him, as he had asked so many people to do, and like so many people she had refused. (Can you (ex)change lives? Can you (ex)change deaths?)

Lord Galen was discoursing upon dreams. "Sometimes," he said, "I want prophetic dreams, lucrative dreams which come without warning. Last year, for example, I woke with a cry of astonishment to hear a voice say: 'The obvious thing at the end of a war as wasteful as this last one is a contract for scrap metal.' It was a revelation – the obvious always is! Within ten days I was negotiating with ten governments to take over their deserted battlefields!"

"Yes, I also used to be scared of snakes," Max was saying, "until I went to India to study. In the *ashram* there was a king cobra with a mate and they were quite tame; they came out at dusk and drank milk from a saucer with little flickering tongues. You could describe them as good-humoured when not alarmed and quite unaggressive. But in another part of India they killed snakes and there I noticed how faithful the female was and how deadly. She always returns to avenge her mate, and for days after a male has been killed the whole place is in a state of acute anxiety waiting for her certain reappearance. Usually she comes three or four days after the killing of her mate. They say that this is the better to plan her ambush because she is careful to execute her retaliation according to a set plan. She lies in wait in some place where people are bound to pass – on a thoroughfare or pathway, in a kitchen or at a shrine. If any unwary person approaches she strikes with all her might. But I was very impressed by the anxiety with which the whole household awaited her coming. My teachers used this as a metaphor. The state of watchfulness as if for this second coming!"

The noise of the music rolled over his words and he felt snatches of sleep invading his whole consciousness in little paroxysms of pleasure. The collision of different languages superposed and mingled gave a wonderful barbaric note to the fair. One could imagine whole conversations when one did not understand what was being said.

Who is your friend over there? The cannibal one?

Death!

He looks rather nice.

He improves on acquaintance. The man with a pocketful of deaths.

I thought he looked familiar.

The Prince's car was full of small gipsies – they had asked for a ride and were being driven over the bridge and around the leafy roads with their dapples of frenzied light. The great engine purred, soft as elephant fur, emissary from the world of Pelf and Vox Pop and processed citizen. "Everyone is here save the lovers and Smirgel," said the Préfet on a note of deep anxiety, as he wished to begin his alembicated discourse well before the advance into the caves.

"They will come," said Felix soothingly. And truth to tell they were not far off. As for the lovers, they had elected to ride up from the sea and with the falling of darkness had reached Remoulins when the meandering roads led them steadily towards the bridge; from time to time through the forest they caught glimpses of insinuating light against the distant sky. Soon the distant clamour of mandolins would greet them. They advanced like riders in a dream, his arm through hers. They had decided to separate for a while, perhaps for several months, in order to give themselves the possibility of concentrating all their forces upon the book which he had decided to begin at long last. But this could not be done without a finalising meeting with Sutcliffe for whom now the enormous sense of utter despondency had once more gained the forefront of his mind – the despair over the inaccessibility of Sabine. As they wound slowly through the dark glades he told her his plan and asked for her permission to execute it.

She was vehemently in favour of it; she felt, in fact, that the whole *oeuvre* for which he was going to try was as much her work, her responsibility, as his – which was indeed the case. To celebrate the mystical marriage of four dimensions with five skandas so to speak. To exemplify in the flesh the royal cobra couple, the king and queen of the affect, of the spiritual world. "My spinal I with her final she." Some of this they tried to express to Sutcliffe who remained somewhat unconvinced. "Very well," he said at last, "on condition that you don't write like a hundred garbage cans. But first we should clap eyes on the treasure, no? To console ourselves against the cold and damp of our native island – that barbaric place with its two tribes." The Prince explained the allusion. "At first you have difficulty liking the inhabitants. Then you realise that they come in two sorts, the British and the English. The first are descendants of Calvin, the second descendants of Rupert Brooke! Poets and Idealists against Protestant shop-keepers. Hence the divided voice which so often fills us with dismay. After all, in this hideous war we have just passed through never forget that Halifax would have treated with Hitler: it took Churchill to refuse. England over Britain!" It was one of his favourite themes, and one very congenial to a typically Egyptian temperament. As who should know!

The remaining two persons – Smirgel and Quatrefages – arrived in an old fashioned gig with a somewhat super-annuated horse drawing them. They looked somehow dazed in a vaguely triumphant way, and the German, true to his promise, had brought the Austrian sapper's map of the workings without which all access to the treasure would have proved impossible. But first the warnings, and here the Préfet could afford to wax somewhat rhetorical as he pleaded for care and circumspection and civic respect for the saint – if they managed to locate her. His voice was from time to time drowned by the moan of mandolins. But at long last the great moment announced itself; Cade manifested in a puff of smoke and a flash – an optical illusion which the light created as it flashed among the leaves. He had with him a whole bundle of lottery tickets which he wore over his shoulder like a bandolier. This had been Smirgel's idea. "It would be wise to keep a check on those who go in. The gipsies are such a rabble I am scared to let them in. But if you give them a ticket each we can do a count later on if something goes wrong." There were also torches to be distributed and fairy-lights . . . All these elements had to be coaxed into some sort of order. Slowly the mellifluous periods of the official French wound to a halt.

"And so, my children," – for he could not resist the avuncular note – "let us go in all humility in search of our Saint who alone will secure the well-being of all who live here. Viva Sara!" The cry went off like a pistol shot and for a long moment the music swept upwards towards the sky in a glorious arpeggio while individual voices barked the savage message to the shade of the Saint. "Viva Sara! Viva Sara!" And now the fireworks ranged upon the aqueduct started to splutter and whizz – crowns and globes of spinning light in a deep blue sky. The volume of the music turned itself down and a single plangent woman's voice started to sing a love-song, an Andalusian folk-tune with its curious peristaltic rhythm and alternative breaths suggestive of the human orgasm. Sutcliffe said grimly, "Sex – the human animal's larder." And his double said, "Yes. Or the fatal power-house. We could do so much with it if we learned the code!" But the Prince who had learned of the mortal illness of the Princess and was planning to leave for Cairo at dawn, was thinking of other things – of mortal sin, parodied by illnesses of the physical envelope! He could see so clearly into the future of her death, clearer than any gipsy. On the anniversary of it the telephone smothered in tea-roses – white roses and red. In this way to conspire against console, and hope in their love. Aubrey said, "When we separate shall we correspond, do you think?" Sutcliffe said, "Of course. We mustn't neglect to think of the collected correspondence – an exchange of hiero-glyphs between two cuneiform personages, what? A corres-pondence in Mandarin?"

The procession was forming; at its head would ride the Prince and the Préfet in the royal Daimler; then the official limousine; then the other cars and the ribbon of caravans. At the head of the procession walked the magnificent singing woman-gipsy in all her finery while the cars followed, slowed down to her pace. In this way they covered the quarter of a mile to the cave entry with its ominous hoardings with the inscription DANGER everywhere written large. Here Cade had taken up his position in order to give everyone a ticket before letting them through the barrier. The first cave was vast, like a cathedral, and was rapidly filled. Now it was time to advance down the inner corridors guided by Smirgel and Quatrefages. The lovers gave a shiver of premonition and Blanford thought that if ever he wrote the scene he would say: "It was at this precise moment that reality prime rushed to the aid of fiction and the totally unpredictable began to take place!"